Spirit

OF THE LAW

Praise for Carsen Taite

Best Practice

"I had fun reading this story and watching the final law partner find her true love. If you like a delightful, romantic age-gap tale involving lawyers, you will like *Best Practice*. In fact, I believe you will like all three books in the Legal Affairs series."—*Rainbow Reflections*

"I think this could very well be my favourite book in this series. *Best Practice* is a light and easy opposites-attract age-gap read. It's well-paced and fun, not overly angsty, with just enough tension to be exciting."—*Jude in the Stars*

Drawn

"This book held my attention from start to finish. I'm a huge Taite fan and I love it when she writes lesbian crime romance books. Because Taite knows so much about the law, it gives her books an authentic feel that I love…Ms. Taite builds the relationship between the main characters with a strong bond and excellent chemistry. Both characters are opposites in many ways but their attraction is undeniable and sizzling."— *LezReviewBooks.com*

Out of Practice

"Taite combines legal and relationship drama to create this realistic and deeply enjoyable lesbian romance…The reliably engaging Taite neatly balances romance and red-hot passion with a plausible legal story line, well-drawn characters, and pitch-perfect pacing that culminates in the requisite heartfelt happily-ever-after." —*Publishers Weekly*

"[A] quick read romance that gave me all the good feelings. I recommend to people who like to read about romance, vacations, flings, lawyers, blogging, weddings, friends, fighting the feelings, grand gestures, protesters, and wedding veils."—*Bookvark*

Leading the Witness

"This was an enjoyable read. I recommend this to those who like mystery, suspense, prosecution, investigations, romance, and Balcones bourbon."—*Bookvark*

Practice Makes Perfect

"This book has two fantastic leads, an attention-grabbing plot and that sizzling chemistry that great authors can make jump off the page. While all of Taite's books are fantastic, this one is on that next level. This is a damn good book and I cannot wait to see what is next in this series."—*Romantic Reader Blog*

Pursuit of Happiness

"I like Taite's style of writing. She is consistent in terms of quality and always writes strong female characters that are as intelligent as they are beautiful."—*Lesbian Reading Room*

"I can't believe I'm saying this, but I think Meredith and Stevie are my new favourite couple that Taite's written…They're brilliant, funny, and the chemistry between them is out of control."—*Lesbian Review*

Love's Verdict

"Carsen Taite excels at writing legal thrillers with lesbian main characters using her experience as a criminal defense attorney." —*Lez Review Books*

Outside the Law

"[A] fabulous closing to the Lone Star Law series…Tanner and Sydney's journey back to each other is sweet, sexy and sure to keep you entertained."—*Romantic Reader Blog*

Reasonable Doubt

"Another Carsen Taite novel that kept me on the edge of my seat… [A]n interesting plot with lots of mystery and a bit of thriller as well. The characters were great."—*Danielle Kimerer, Librarian, Reading Public Library*

Lay Down the Law

"Recognized for the pithy realism of her characters and settings drawn from a Texas legal milieu, Taite pays homage to the prime-time soap opera *Dallas* in pairing a cartel-busting U.S. attorney, Peyton Davis, with a charity-minded oil heiress, Lily Gantry." —*Publishers Weekly*

"Suspenseful, intriguingly tense, and with a great developing love story, this book is delightfully solid on all fronts."—*Rainbow Book Reviews*

Courtship

"Taite (*Switchblade*) keeps the stakes high as two beautiful and brilliant women fueled by professional ambitions face daunting emotional choices…As backroom politics, secrets, betrayals, and threats race to be resolved without political damage to the president, the cat-and-mouse relationship game between Addison and Julia has the reader rooting for them. Taite prolongs the fever-pitch tension to the final pages. This pleasant read with intelligent heroines, snappy dialogue, and political suspense will satisfy Taite's devoted fans and new readers alike."—*Publishers Weekly*

Switchblade

"Dallas's intrepid female bounty hunter, Luca Bennett, is back in another adventure. Fantastic! Between her many friends and lovers, her interesting family, her fly by the seat of her pants lifestyle, and a whole host of detractors there is rarely a dull moment." —*Rainbow Book Reviews*

Beyond Innocence

"Taite keeps you guessing with delicious delay until the very last minute…Taite's time in the courtroom lends *Beyond Innocence* a terrific verisimilitude someone not in the profession couldn't impart. And damned if she doesn't make practicing law interesting."
—*Out in Print*

The Best Defense

"Real-life defense attorney Carsen Taite polishes her fifth work of lesbian fiction, *The Best Defense*, with the realism she daily encounters in the office and in the courts. And that polish is something that makes *The Best Defense* shine as an excellent read."
—*Out & About Newspaper*

Nothing but the Truth

"Author Taite is really a Dallas defense attorney herself, and it's obvious her viewpoint adds considerable realism to her story, making it especially riveting as a mystery. I give it four stars out of five."—*Bob Lind, Echo Magazine*

Do Not Disturb

"Taite's tale of sexual tension is entertaining in itself, but a number of secondary characters…add substantial color to romantic inevitability."—*Richard Labonte, Book Marks*

It Should Be a Crime—Lammy Finalist

"Taite, a criminal defense attorney herself, has given her readers a behind the scenes look at what goes on during the days before a trial. Her descriptions of lawyer/client talks, investigations, police procedures, etc. are fascinating. Taite keeps the action moving, her characters clear, and never allows her story to get bogged down in paperwork. *It Should Be a Crime* has a fast-moving plot and some extraordinarily hot sex."—*Just About Write*

By the Author

Truelesbianlove.com

It Should Be a Crime

Do Not Disturb

Nothing but the Truth

The Best Defense

Beyond Innocence

Rush

Courtship

Reasonable Doubt

Without Justice

Sidebar

A More Perfect Union

Love's Verdict

Pursuit of Happiness

Leading the Witness

Drawn

Double Jeopardy (novella in Still Not Over You)

Spirit of the Law

The Luca Bennett Mystery Series:

Slingshot

Battle Axe

Switchblade

Bow and Arrow (novella in Girls with Guns)

Lone Star Law Series:

Lay Down the Law   Letter of the Law

Above the Law   Outside the Law

Legal Affairs Romances

Practice Makes Perfect   Best Practice

Out of Practice

Visit us at www.boldstrokesbooks.com

SPIRIT
OF THE LAW

by
Carsen Taite

2021

SPIRIT OF THE LAW
© 2021 BY CARSEN TAITE. ALL RIGHTS RESERVED.

ISBN 13: 978-1-63555-766-4

THIS TRADE PAPERBACK ORIGINAL IS PUBLISHED BY
BOLD STROKES BOOKS, INC.
P.O. BOX 249
VALLEY FALLS, NY 12185

FIRST EDITION: FEBRUARY 2021

CREDITS
EDITOR: CINDY CRESAP
PRODUCTION DESIGN: STACIA SEAMAN
COVER DESIGN BY TAMMY SEIDICK

Acknowledgments

This entire book was written during the pandemic. Thankfully, I had a deadline because without that kind of accountability, the distractions of 2020 threatened to derail the creative process entirely. I am writing these acknowledgments on the eve of the 2020 election and have no idea what the world will look like when this book finds itself in your hands, but I know this: our stories are more important now than ever, and I am incredibly grateful for the opportunity to write about our lives and our loves, and I will never take this privilege for granted, no matter what the future holds.

Thanks to Rad and Sandy and the entire crew at Bold Strokes Books for running a publishing house that manages to be both professional and nurturing at the same time—I'm proud to call BSB home. To my editor, Cindy, your keen eye always makes me look better, and you deserve all the See's Candies in the land! Tammy, thank you for another striking cover.

Special shout-outs to Georgia for our daily check-ins (especially meaningful this year), Ruth for her magical blurb stylings, and my bestie Paula for reading every draft, brainstorming plot points, and being an amazing friend. To the rest of my posse, I can't wait until we can meet in person for martinis/wine/old fashioneds, big laughs, and deep conversation.

Spirit of the Law is a bit outside the box for me. While still centered around the law with all the tenets that anchor our justice system, this story also explores the value of believing in truths we can't see but that are often more real than the cold, hard facts we call evidence. I hope you enjoy a little dose of the unworldly with your romantic intrigue.

Thanks to my wife, Lainey, for always believing in my dreams even when they involve sacrificing our time together. I had a blast brainstorming this story with you. I couldn't live this dream without you and I wouldn't want to.

And to my loyal readership, thank you, thank you, thank you. Every time you purchase one of my stories, you give me the gift of allowing me to make a living doing what I love. Thanks for taking this journey with me.

To Lainey. My kindred spirit.

Chapter One

W hat if they lock you up and don't let you out until you all agree?"

Summer Byrne shook her head at the question, the tenth or so one her daughter, Faith, had posed since she'd informed her she might be late picking her up from school that afternoon. "Doubtful. Besides, it's Friday. Even if I get picked for a jury, and that's a big if, it's probably going to be for something minor and the case will be wrapped up before the weekend. Attorneys don't like to have a verdict hanging out over the weekend."

"How do you know so much about being on juries?" Faith asked.

Summer's stomach churned at the question, but thankfully, she pulled into the driveway for Faith's school—the perfect moment to change the subject. "Hey, kiddo, time to get your learnin' on."

Faith sighed as she gathered her things. "Mom, please don't try to sound cool. It's not working for you."

Summer laughed at Faith's serious expression. Faith's first year in middle school meant Summer was ancient and out of touch instead of the cool mom she'd been all through elementary school. Summer wrote off the change in her status as a natural by-product of having an almost teenager. At least she'd never be as decidedly uncool as her own overly formal mother who insisted on setting out cookies and milk for Summer's friends long after they were old enough to drive and make out in the back seats of their boyfriends' cars.

"Thanks for being concerned about my welfare. Much appreciated. Now go, so I can get to the courthouse and be the nerd that I am. I'll text you when I know if I've been picked."

She watched Faith go, a little jealous of her middle school regimen. She'd been doing temp work for the last few months since they'd moved back to Dallas—boring, administrative stuff for various businesses—and the lack of any kind of consistent routine was starting to wear her down. Routine kept her focused, kept her from getting restless, and kept her mind from wandering. Right now, she could use a healthy dose of same old same old, but the jury summons in her purse was about to wreck that. Hopefully, she'd be in and out within an hour, two tops.

This courthouse was like others she'd frequented, a combination of anxious and overbearing people mixed with a cacophony of sounds humming all around her. The central jury room was marked with a large sign, and she entered the room and took a seat toward the back, seeking respite from the buzz of nervous energy in the room. It didn't work. She'd brought a paperback, a mystery she'd swiped from her grandmother's collection, but after reading the same paragraph a dozen times with little to no comprehension, she shoved it in her bag and gave in to the unspoken voices in the room.

"If I don't get back to the restaurant, I'm going to get fired."

"They don't even reimburse you the full price of parking."

"Should I tell the bailiff I have a conviction on my record

or should I wait and tell the judge? They're not going to pick someone with a record, are they?"

Summer breathed in and out slowly, seeking some sense of calm as a shield against the onslaught of other people's thoughts, but it was her against at least a hundred other folks. By the time they called her name, she was weak with resistance.

"Summer Byrne, please report to the bailiff."

The woman calling her name pointed to a man in uniform standing by the door they'd entered. Summer hesitated for a moment, praying the bailiff was simply going to tell her how to claim her parking voucher. She tentatively approached him while the rest of the room resumed its low buzz. "Hi, I'm Summer Byrne. They just called my name."

He consulted his clipboard. "Fourth floor. Court twelve."

Summer frowned as she tried to digest the terse phrases. "Excuse me?"

He repeated the same information and Summer resigned herself to the fact she was moving on to the next phase. The lobby was crammed with people waiting for the elevator, and the last thing she wanted was to be stuffed in a tiny space full of thoughts that weren't her own, so she spent a moment searching until she found the stairs. By flight three, she was winded and vowed to get more exercise if the universe would only let her have the strength to make it to the next floor alive. She emerged from the stairwell in time to hear her name being called out by another uniformed man who was guarding a large plastic trash bin full of clipboards.

He shoved a clipboard her way as she approached. "You're number twenty-two. Fill this out and bring it back." He immediately shouted out another name and pulled another clipboard from the stack.

Terseness was a systemic issue here. One more big

city thing Summer would have to get used to. She glanced over the questionnaire. She'd seen plenty like it before, but there was definitely something different about viewing it from the perspective of the answerer of questions instead of the evaluator of the answers. She zoomed through most of the questions, leaving blank her response for spouse's name and occupation—thanks, Universe, for reminding her of her perpetual single status and the fact she hadn't yet found a permanent job.

When she reached the questions about whether she or any of her family members worked in law enforcement, she tapped the pen against her clipboard and contemplated her response. Technically and literally, the answer was no, but it wasn't an entirely honest answer. If she were to be completely honest, her answer would only invite follow-up questions. Questions she didn't want to have to answer at all, let alone in front of a bunch of strangers in open court. She weighed the question, examined it from all angles, and ultimately decided based on the tense of the question, she was going to stick with a literal answer to the straightforward inquiry, and she left the box unchecked.

A long twenty minutes later, she filed into the courtroom with the rest of the potential jurors and took her seat in the first spot on the second row—right on the edge of the safety zone for a misdemeanor case where the first six people on the panel who weren't struck for cause or for some gut feeling on the part of either side would wind up in the jury box hearing testimony in this trial. Once she was settled into her seat, she focused her attention toward the front of the room where the judge, a tall, slender Black woman, stood at the bench, towering over several people who she presumed were attorneys and the defendant standing at tables situated so the chairs faced the jury box.

"I wonder what he did."

"Looks guilty to me."

"Which one's the defense attorney? Doesn't matter. They both look like trouble."

"I hope we get a break for lunch."

"Wow, who's the hot juror in the second row?"

The last voice jarred Summer out of her reverie and she turned to see a tall, striking woman walking down the aisle toward the front of the courtroom. She locked eyes with Summer for a moment, and Summer spotted a trace of a smile before she sat at the table closest to her side of the room. Every other voice blurred into the background, and Summer was riveted by the woman's controlled but engaging smile and her piercing dark brown eyes. Faith would describe her as dope or some other resurrection of retro cool, and if that meant intoxicating, then Faith would be right. The women's suit looked perfectly tailored and every hair in her cropped cut was perfectly coiffed. Summer ran a hand through her own hair, conscious she could use a haircut and wondering if the small stain from this morning's coffee on the sleeve of her sweater was visible from the front of the courtroom.

"Good morning," the judge said. "My name is Judge Audra Dewitt. Thank you all for showing up today to perform your civic duty. Without your participation, the justice system would grind to a halt."

Summer listened as the judge continued with her introduction and outline of the type of case they would be deciding if they were selected to be on the jury, and focused her attention on shutting out the anxious thoughts of the people around her that ranged from dread about having to decide someone's fate to fear that missing work to help so-called justice would mean the inability to put food on the table. Even when the other voices faded to the background, she didn't hear another single thought from sharp-dressed Brown Eyes in the front of the room, and that piqued her curiosity.

"Representing Mr. Jex, the defendant, is Tom Moss," Judge Dewitt said. "And for the state, we have assistant district attorney, Ben Green..." the judge paused while the pudgy, slightly rumpled man seated next to Brown Eyes waved at them, "and ADA Owen Lassiter."

Owen rose slightly at the introduction and nodded at the assembled jurors. Deferential, but still powerful, and Summer found herself nodding back, and the simple act was like a tractor beam, drawing Owen's attention to her. They locked eyes again, and Summer felt stripped and vulnerable under Owen's steady gaze.

The entire exchange lasted less than a minute, but Summer's entire body was buzzing after. Whatever had just happened between them was important, monumental even, and she couldn't discern if it was good or bad, but it definitely wasn't neutral. Maybe jury duty wouldn't be so bad after all.

❖

Owen Lassiter crouched over the desk in the DA workroom and shifted through the questionnaires, cross-checking them with the meticulous chart her second chair, Ben, had prepared while she'd been questioning the jury panel. Part of jury selection was math. If each side had three strikes and six people wound up on the jury, then ostensibly the first twelve panelists were the only ones that mattered. But the judge had already agreed to release some jurors for cause—lack of child care, insisted they couldn't be fair given their background, etc., which left the attorneys looking deeper into the available jurors, leaving them to make some educated guesses about how to use their preemptory strikes. The better the guess, the more likely you could net the people most sympathetic to your case, and Owen was known throughout the courthouse for being the jury whisperer. She had a perfect trial record because of it. Each side had had an hour to ask the panel questions, and now they had thirty minutes to list their strikes. In another room, the defense attorneys were engaged in the same guessing game. The key was to not only strike the jurors you didn't want, but to anticipate who the other side would strike so that you didn't use up your strikes on people they were going to get rid of anyway.

Ben shoved one of the questionnaires toward her. "This guy hates cops."

"Hate's a strong word, Ben."

"Strongly dislikes, then. Every time you brought up how the arrest went down, he looked like he'd eaten a lemon. Besides, there's the issue of his brother getting arrested last year. I don't care what he said to Dewitt about how he could put aside his own experience, he's waiting for the perfect opportunity to bust some balls."

He was right and Owen knew it, but part of her job as the chief of the misdemeanor courts was to teach the prosecutors she supervised, and getting Ben to articulate his process was key to her success. The primary evidence in this case was the police officer's testimony, making it paramount to root out any bias against cops. "Okay, put him down as a no. Who else?"

Ben rattled off a few more names and they settled on another strike among the first twenty jurors on the panel. Then he tapped his finger on juror number twenty-two. "She looks okay on paper."

And gorgeous in real life. Known for being unflappable in the courtroom, Owen had almost lost it when caught in juror twenty-two's gaze. She glanced at the name on the questionnaire. *Summer Byrne.* She schooled her face into what she hoped was a neutral expression. "She barely said anything."

"She said she could be fair when we polled the panel, and she sounded sincere. Nothing of concern on the questionnaire."

Owen looked at the form, impressed by the beautiful cursive handwriting that seemed so old school and yet endearing. Ostensibly, Summer Byrne was the perfect neutral juror, but Owen had a feeling Summer wasn't quite what she appeared to be, although she couldn't articulate a reason why. She reached for Ben's chart. "Who's number twenty-three?"

"Lance Goetz. He's got a family member who's been arrested before. If you're choosing between these two, I'd strike Goetz."

It was an easy decision, and Owen wrote Goetz's name on the list without hesitation. Bonus points that she'd get to spend the rest of the trial looking at Summer, provided the defense didn't use one of their strikes on her. She handed the completed form to Ben so he could turn it over to the bailiff, and after checking to see that she still had a few minutes before they were to reconvene, she walked out of the room to stretch.

The hallway outside of the courtroom was teeming with jurors waiting to hear their fate, but she ducked her head and kept walking as if she didn't see them, trying to act like she couldn't hear them as well. Still snippets of conversation floated their way to her ears.

"I have places to be."

"This is a waste of time."

"I wonder if the cafeteria is any good."

She resisted responding to the last one—only if you know what to order. She kept walking, but then one voice stood out.

"I told you I have jury duty today...No, I don't know when I'll be done. You should probably not count on me to show up. It's not like I did this on purpose. Look, I have to go.

If something happens and I'm available this afternoon, I'll let you know."

Owen slowed her pace and shot a quick glance toward the voice, confirming it was Summer talking to someone on the phone. Eavesdropping on jurors' private conversations wasn't something she did on a regular basis, but she told herself this was different. The level of tension she heard in Summer's voice would have captured anyone's attention, and she was merely being a concerned citizen. When Summer looked up and met her eyes, all reason faded. She should exercise some discretion and look away, but she couldn't help but linger for the chance at getting another glimpse at those captivating blue eyes outside of the confines of the courtroom. It didn't hurt that Summer stared right back as she disconnected the call.

"Well, that was embarrassing."

Uh-oh. Owen paused her stride at the remark, half-hoping it wasn't directed at her, but she knew it was. Sidelong glances at a potential juror was one thing, but she couldn't be seen speaking to her, not until after the trial was over if Summer was selected to be on this jury. She flashed what she hoped was a reassuring smile, nodded, and kept walking. It wasn't easy to walk away from a beautiful woman who appeared to be in distress, and it took all of her resistance not to look back over her shoulder, but she held strong. Damn.

When she reached the stairwell, she heard a voice calling her name. She turned to see her best friend, Mary Pierce, running up behind her, puffing from the effort.

"You must be in trial mode. I yelled your name like a dozen times," Mary said.

"Maybe I was just ignoring you."

"As if. Seriously, though, I know it's a big case and you're probably deep in thought about strategy."

Owen sighed. Mary had been ribbing her for days

about her plan to beef up the training of the misdemeanor prosecutors under her command. She'd pledged to try a case with one of them a week to demonstrate the techniques she'd used to amass a perfect record of not guilty verdicts. So far, her record was intact, even though there had been a few close calls over the past month from junior prosecutors who seemed determined to blow the cases she handpicked to try. "I think I can handle it. Ben seems like he knows what he's doing, generally speaking."

"Then leave him to it and come to lunch with me. I want to hear all about how you snagged the Adams case from Ron," she said, referring to a highly anticipated upcoming trial involving the murder of the county commissioner's wife.

"I didn't snag anything. The case was over his head and he mouthed off to the press, so M—Ms. Rivera pulled Ron and bumped me up to first chair." She stumbled over the elected district attorney's name, almost slipping by using her first name instead of the customary formality.

"Who's going to try it with you?"

"Angling for the job?"

"Maybe. The mini-cap I had set for next month fell apart, which means I have the time. Unless there's someone else you have in mind."

"Let me talk to Rivera. She's taking a special interest in this case and I don't want to do anything unexpected."

"Got it. Did you hear there was another mugging last night? This one was downtown?"

"I saw that," Owen said. "That's the sixth one since the first of the month. I heard DPD is assigning a bunch of undercover officers to try to catch this guy, but he keeps striking in different places, so it's pretty much a guessing game as to where he's going to show up next."

"That's a case I want to try. I hope they catch him soon."

"Agreed."

"Great. Now for lunch."

"No can do." Owen glanced at her phone. "Time to find out who wound up on the jury. I love this part."

Mary laughed. "Said no one else ever." She play-pushed Owen's shoulder. "Go. Be the nerd you are and win Ben's case for him."

Owen laughed, but secretly she wished Mary would quit ribbing her about her win record, not because she wasn't proud of it, but she feared too much talk would jinx her success. She spent the few minutes it took her to walk back to the courtroom centering her mind on the case ahead. Yes, it was a simple possession of marijuana case, and if convicted, the defendant was likely to get probation, but the key to her success had always been the way she treated every case like it was the most serious one that would cross her desk and knowing how to pick her battles. This case had the opportunity for some great teachable moments, but it should be a slam dunk if bad mojo didn't get in the way.

As she walked into the courtroom, she scanned the crowd to size up the panel one last time, but when her gaze settled on juror number twenty-two, her body hummed and she couldn't help but smile. If Summer wound up on the jury, this case could wind up being way more interesting than she'd imagined.

CHAPTER TWO

"I cannot believe I wound up on this jury."

In an instinctively polite move, Summer nodded at juror four, the twenty-something woman seated across from her. Brittany…yes, that was her name. Satisfied she now knew all she wanted to about her, Summer quickly ducked her head back into the book she'd brought to pass the time. An hour ago, they'd been summoned back into the courtroom, sworn into service, read the charges, and then given an abbreviated, early lunch break. She'd found a secluded spot in the far corner of the basement cafeteria to devour the not so fresh sandwich she'd purchased, but there really wasn't any place in the entire building that wasn't riddled with other people's emotions, and that fact was becoming even clearer now that she was back in the small jury room with five of her peers.

She'd been listening to Brittany complain for the last thirty minutes, and her whine was beginning to wear. Summer resisted pointing out that if she'd spoken up this much during jury selection, maybe she wouldn't have wound up serving, but she didn't want to engage. She could sympathize, though. She didn't want to be on the jury either. For so many reasons. Way more important reasons than the missed spa day Brittany had mentioned, but she wasn't about to air her grievances in this group of strangers.

"How long do you think it will take?"

"A day. Two at the most." Summer spoke the words before thinking, and she immediately spotted the light in the woman's eyes, like she realized she'd lucked into someone knowledgeable about the court system. She sought to minimize. "I really have no idea."

"Sounds like you have *some* idea."

"Yeah, it does." The second voice was the man who'd talked a lot during voir dire, juror eighteen—Wayne. He'd been acting like he didn't want to be here, but it was clear he craved the attention that came with being selected to serve on the jury. He poured his second cup of coffee and settled into the seat next to hers.

Summer shifted in her chair. "Just guessing. You know, based on what I've seen on TV. They read out a list of witnesses and there weren't very many. It's a misdemeanor case and the judge said probation was an option. Doesn't sound like anything earth-shattering to me."

"True," Brittany said. "I mean, either he had the drugs or he didn't. I'm thinking he did."

"We're not supposed to talk about the case."

The three of them turned toward the door of the room and Summer felt a rush of relief. The man entering the room, Tucker, had been on the first row during voir dire, seated next to Brittany. Like her, he hadn't said much during the proceeding, but Summer was certain he was a gentle, thoughtful soul. She felt his stress about having to sit in judgment, but also his strong enough sense of duty not to try to use that stress to get out of his civic responsibility. She watched him settle into a chair across from her and meet her eyes with an inquisitive expression that told her she'd been staring. *Careful, Byrne.* She nodded to acknowledge his words. "You're right. We shouldn't be discussing anything about the case."

"Well, can we at least talk about how bad this coffee is?" Wayne said, raising his mug. "I mean, this case better not last long or I'll have to find a way to sneak a thermos of my personal brew into this place."

"How about we share a little bit about ourselves," Tucker said. "I've lived in Dallas my entire life, but this is my first time on a jury. I don't have a clue what to expect. I'm an organist for a church in Uptown."

His warm, friendly voice almost compelled Summer to jump in next, but she resisted the urge. She wasn't here to make friends. These people were a group of strangers who would bond for a day or so and then go home, likely never to see each other again. She'd share as little as possible with them lest she risk everything she'd put into making a new start for herself and Faith.

She needn't have worried. Wayne was eager to do all the talking.

"I'm the CEO of my own start-up restaurant delivery service," he said, proceeding to list all the ways his business was better than another one in town. "I took several law classes in business school so if we get to anything complicated, I'm sure I can help out."

Summer caught the rest of the group rolling their eyes as Wayne wrangled for a nomination to foreman when the time came to make the choice. Thankfully, at that moment, the bailiff showed up at the door and told them the judge was ready for them to reenter the courtroom.

Everyone stood as they entered the room and filed into their seats in the jury box. The courtroom looked different from the jury box than it had when they were sitting in the gallery. Once they were seated, the rest of the people in the room followed suit, and Summer glanced at everyone in the room. Owen and Ben sat at the table closest to them. Ben was anxious, the nerves emanating off of him in strong waves, but Owen was calm and collected. The defendant was huddled close to his attorney and they appeared to be in a deliberative discussion. She wasn't able to make out words from their whispers, only a contentious tone. The defense attorney ultimately shushed his client with a stern look, and Summer had a flash of the pain it caused the defendant to be silenced so abruptly.

"Is the state ready to proceed?" the judge asked.

Ben rose from his chair. "We are, Your Honor." He pushed off from the table and walked a few feet toward them and cleared his throat. "Ladies and gentlemen of the jury, I'd like to begin by thanking you for your service. Today, you will hear a case with facts that sound routine. The police pull over a motorist on a routine traffic stop, but once they speak with the defendant, they realize something more is happening based on the defendant's demeanor, the way he responds to simple questions, the way he shifts his eyesight to indicate his concern the stop might escalate into more than just a speeding ticket or some other simple violation. You will hear testimony that the defendant was in possession of an illegal substance, marijuana, and it was right there in the passenger compartment of the vehicle."

He kept talking, but the rest of his words fell away as Summer felt a strong pull to look at the defendant, Jex, who was staring straight ahead, looking decidedly uncomfortable at being the topic of conversation.

"I didn't do it."

The statement was definitive and clear, and Summer instantly knew he was telling the truth even if no one else in the courtroom heard Jex's words. She barely listened to the rest of Ben's statement, keeping her eyes trained on Jex, looking for any additional sign to support the overwhelming feeling everything that was being said about him was dead wrong. He looked young, almost too young to be tried as an adult, but she supposed if this were really a big deal, they'd be in a felony trial and Jex would be facing jail time. Still, he looked awfully nervous for a guy who was looking at probation at worst, but she knew above anything else he didn't do what he was accused of, and she hoped the trial would bear out his innocence.

❖

Three hours later, Summer took her seat with the others in the jury room and tried not to yawn. The level of angst in the courtroom had her on edge, and she was thankful the testimony was over, and they were one step closer to going home.

Wayne took the seat at the head of the table and called them to order. "The judge said we should elect a foreperson before we do anything else. Would anyone like to volunteer?"

Summer could tell he was itching to fill the role, and she didn't care either way. As long as they all reached the same conclusion, it didn't matter who tallied the votes.

"She should do it."

Summer whipped her head to the left and saw Yolanda, the only other woman besides her and Brittany on the jury, pointing in her direction. Yolanda was a schoolteacher nearing retirement, and up to this moment, hadn't said more than a few words. "What?"

"You seem to know a lot about courtroom stuff," Yolanda said as she scanned the faces of the rest of the group, daring them to question her. I think you'd do a great job." She raised her hand. "I vote yes. Who's with me?"

Summer watched as the rest of the jurors raised their hands, some, like Wayne, more slowly than others. Resigned to her fate, she pulled one of the pads of paper on the table toward her. "I think the first order of business should be to review the evidence."

"How about we take a vote?" Wayne said. "I'm pretty sure I know how we're all going to vote."

The rest of the jurors voiced their approval. Summer briefly closed her eyes and mentally counted the five guilty verdicts scrawled on snips of paper she was about to tear from the pad. No sense wasting paper on this round. "Okay. Let's do a show of hands. Everyone who votes guilty?"

Three hands shot into the air and two more tentatively joined them. Summer watched her fellow jurors smile at each other in celebration of the fact they were about to go home. She hated to kill their joy, but she'd hate herself more if she didn't follow her gut. "And not guilty?" She slowly raised her hand as the rest of the jurors stared at her in disbelief.

"Seriously? You were in the room, right?" Wayne wasn't holding back. "It's freaking Friday afternoon. Don't you have somewhere you'd rather be?"

Summer stared him down and then looked at the rest of the group. Yolanda's expression said she was reconsidering the prudence of recruiting Summer to the position of foreperson, but it didn't matter. She'd make the same decision either way. "Yes, I do, but we swore an oath to follow the law. I don't think Mr. Jex should've been arrested in the first place."

"So, now the guy with marijuana in his car is *Mister* Jex, worthy of our respect?" Wayne said. "You don't think he's guilty, but you don't really know, do you?" *"She probably thinks the guy who broke into my car last week deserves a prize for his efforts."*

Summer started to answer the unspoken question before

she caught herself. Instead she took a different approach. "You're right. I don't know, but I want to be sure, like beyond a reasonable doubt sure, before I sign my name to a verdict. How about we take a minute to review the evidence and the instructions and then take another vote?"

Wayne sighed. "Do we have a choice?"

Yolanda jabbed a finger at him. "I want to go home too, but there's no need to be mean about it. The sooner we review everything, the quicker we'll get out of here. Is everyone okay with that?"

With a few grunts and groans, everyone agreed, and Yolanda motioned to Summer to begin. She cleared her throat and picked up her pen. "Officer Rawlings said he was driving down Mockingbird Lane when he spotted Jex's car. He said he noticed it because Jex was weaving in traffic. He turned on his camera and followed him for a quarter mile, and then activated his siren and pulled him over."

"So far, so good," Wayne said.

"I don't recall the video showing any weaving," Summer said, repeating the claim the defense attorney made during his closing argument, making a note on the pad in front of her. "But we can watch it again if we need to."

"The cop said he probably got his driving under control when he realized he was being followed," Wayne said.

"That's convenient."

Summer turned to look at the unfamiliar voice of juror seven, Ian, who up to now hadn't said a word. He was young, probably around Brittany's age. "Care to elaborate?"

Ian shifted in his seat. "Uh, look, I voted guilty because he had the pot in his car, so he's guilty of that, right? But face it, cops pull people over all the time just looking for something wrong." *It happened to me last month. Luckily, I didn't have any on me at the time.*

"He's right," Brittany said. "But that's their job, right?"

Summer set her pen down. "Let's talk about that. If the stop itself wasn't legal, then we're done here. It doesn't matter what they found in the car." She picked up the jury instructions they'd been given. "It says so right here."

"I don't care what that says, the case wouldn't have made it this far if there weren't a good reason for the officer to arrest this guy in the first place," Wayne said. "My vote stands."

"Tell us what you mean," Yolanda said to Summer.

Summer took a moment to frame her thoughts in layman's terms. "It's like both attorneys said. The first step is probable cause. The officer has to have a reasonable belief that the defendant, Jex, committed a crime. He has to have that to justify pulling him over and asking him questions, asking him to step out of the car, and detaining him on the side of the road while he looks around in the car."

Yolanda nodded. "Okay, that makes sense. So, no weaving, no probable cause. And if it's not on the video, we only have the officer's word."

"Which should be plenty," Wayne said. "He explained that people start driving correctly when they know they're being followed. Happens all the time."

"Okay," Yolanda said. "Assuming that's true, what's next?"

All eyes turned to Summer, and she made a show of looking at the jury instructions, but she already knew the answer. "Next we look at the search itself and why the officer determined it was necessary to search the car, what he found, and where he found it."

Wayne snorted. "Jex was fidgeting. He looked nervous and his eyes were red. Put that with the weaving and it was perfectly reasonable for the officer to assume he was a druggie."

"Assumptions aren't facts," Tucker interjected. "People

assume a lot of things that simply aren't true." *"Everyone at my church assumes I'm straight."*

"Whatever," Wayne said, his tone abrasive. "Those are the facts." *"Let's take another vote and get the hell out of here. Please let these people wise up."*

"You want facts? I'll give you facts," Yolanda replied, and she started ticking off points with her fingers. "One, Jex was driving his cousin's car and he'd never driven it before, which could account for the weaving. Two, he'd just broken up with his girlfriend and he said he had been crying. There's your red eye explanation. Three, I get nervous when I get pulled over by a cop even when I haven't done anything wrong. Cops make people nervous even if you like them." *"Remember that time I'd had one too many and tried to drive to my sister's and hit the mailbox next door."*

Summer watched the back-and-forth, silently rooting for Yolanda's argument to win Wayne over, but she knew there was little chance of that since he seemed entrenched in his desire to get to a quick guilty. Time to move on. "Let's talk about where the drugs were found in the vehicle."

"What difference does it make?" Wayne said. "No one disputes they were there."

"It makes a difference if Jex didn't have care, custody, and control of them." Summer listed her points. "The car wasn't his, and according to him and his cousin, it was his first time driving it. If the drugs were in a part of the car out of his reach, then who's to say he even knew they were there?"

"If they belonged to the cousin, he should do the right thing and step up to take the blame," Brittany said.

"You're assuming they know what the right thing is," Wayne said.

"You're assuming either of these boys knew the drugs were there." Summer knew she sounded crazy. Who wouldn't believe a couple of nineteen-year-olds had some pot and got caught with it? It wasn't like it didn't happen all the time, but this was different. Maybe the cousin was lying and the pot was his, but Jex was telling the truth. Too bad gut feelings and invisible voices weren't admissible evidence she could whip out for the rest of the jurors to consider. She took another tack.

"Even if Jex's cousin knew the pot was there and wasn't big enough to admit it, that still doesn't conclusively establish Jex knew it was there, let alone had access to it." She started digging through the box of exhibits from the trial. "Here," she said, holding up a diagram of the Honda CRV Jex had been driving when he was pulled over. She stabbed her finger at the console in the back seat. "Here's where the officer says he found the drugs." She held her forefinger on the spot and spread her hand so her pinkie was touching the driver's seat. "It's quite a distance from there to the front seat."

The rest of the jurors crowded around the table and stared at her hand on the diagram, and Summer held it there, cocking her head at a faint voice slowly whooshing through the quiet. She looked around. No one's lips were moving, but she met the eyes of Ian, who'd gotten quiet as the conversation had progressed. *"Don't get involved. I need to get to work on time tonight or I'll get fired."*

Summer briefly closed her eyes and sent a silent message back. *"Do the right thing and everything else will work out."* She opened her eyes to find Ian staring intently at her and she wondered if the message landed. She didn't have to wonder long.

"I have this same car," Ian said, flinching slightly as all eyes turned his way. Summer offered him an encouraging smile and he pressed on. "There's no way anyone in the driver's seat could reach into that back console without climbing into the back seat."

Summer looked at the faces of the other jurors, which were more thoughtful than dismissive for the first time since they'd started deliberating.

"Maybe he didn't know it was there."

"I guess it's possible."

"It wasn't his car, after all."

Yolanda summed it up best, and she did it out loud. "And that, folks, is reasonable doubt."

❖

Owen looked up from the police report she was reading. "Stop pacing. You're driving me crazy."

Ben paused for a moment and resumed his back and forth across the small space of the DA workroom. "What's taking so long? This should be an open-and-shut case."

He was right. There had been a total of three witnesses and very little other evidence to review. A simple traffic stop led to the discovery of marijuana in the defendant's car. Jex's bullshit excuse that the car and therefore the pot wasn't his was the predictable explanation of every other defendant in the exact same situation, but reasonable people didn't fall for that argument. Owen understood the jury wanting to discuss the case because the judge had told them to do so, but considering the straightforward facts, she would've expected a verdict within the hour. It had been three hours and the clock was inching toward five p.m. Any minute now, Judge Dewitt would send the bailiff in to see if there was a chance they would reach a verdict today or if they should hold the case over the weekend and resume on Monday, which would spell disaster both for the verdict and for the havoc it would wreak on her schedule. What was the holdup?

As if in answer to her question, Landry, the bailiff, poked

his head in the door. "Light's on. I'm headed back there." He popped out again before she could ask any questions.

"Do you think it's the verdict?" Ben asked.

"Better be," Owen muttered under her breath. Louder, she said, "Let's go find out." She stood and pulled her jacket off the back of the chair and slipped it on. Her afternoon had been a total waste. Normally, she would've spent the time planning for next week or finishing up evaluations for one of the many prosecutors under her supervision, but today she'd sat stewing in the tiny DA workroom shared by the three prosecutors assigned to court twelve, pretending to pore over investigative notes for the Adams trial while she pondered why this jury was taking so damn long to decide this uncomplicated case. Time to get answers.

Except for the defendant, his attorney, and Landry, the courtroom was deserted, which was typical for a Friday afternoon. Owen nodded at opposing counsel and joined Ben at counsel table, resisting the urge to pace the floor while they waited for the jury to enter the room. A moment later, Judge Dewitt appeared in the doorway behind the bench, shrugging her way into her robe. "Any last-minute issues before we bring the jury in?"

"If it's a one-word verdict, are we staying over this evening or starting back up on Monday?" Moss asked. "I only ask because my wife made reservations for our anniversary at the Mansion, and if I'm not going to make it, I'd like to give her time to find someone to take my place."

"Now that's a meal you don't want to miss," Dewitt said. "I'm thinking I should hold you in contempt, have Landry here take you into custody, and take your place."

"She would probably enjoy that very much. I love food as much as the next person, but a seven-course tasting menu seems a little painful to me."

"Prepare yourself, Mr. Moss. We're not staying over tonight."

Owen stared hard at the judge, impatient with the casual conversation and determined to read Dewitt's body language. Were they not staying late because the case would be over or did the judge simply want to let the jury go home for the weekend? She'd just as soon go straight into the punishment phase of the case. It would likely only take a bit longer, and then her schedule would be clear for next week. Plus, it was almost never a good idea to have a two-day break in proceedings. People started thinking, reflecting on the decision they'd made and sometimes second-guessing. If they started to regret finding the defendant guilty, they might try to make up for it by imposing a token punishment, like time served or a light probation.

"Go ahead and bring them in, Mr. Landry," Dewitt said, breaking into her obsessive thoughts.

A moment later, the jury filed in, their eyes down and their pace quiet. They settled into their seats in a different order than they'd filed in, and it took a moment for Owen to spot Summer. She'd made a point of connecting with her during the testimony and closing arguments, partly to foster a connection that might lead to a guilty verdict, but mostly because she was smokin' hot. Right now, she'd settle for some sign, from Summer or anyone else on the jury, to give her a clue as to how they'd decided the case. She didn't have to wait long.

"Ladies and gentlemen of the jury. I understand you've reached a verdict?" Judge Dewitt asked.

Owen's mouth went dry when Summer stood and said, "We have, Your Honor."

"On the single count of possession of marijuana, what is your verdict?"

Owen held her breath.

"We find the defendant, Nathan Jex, not guilty."

"So say you all?"

The jurors nodded, even the outspoken big guy who worked in sales. Despite his agreement with the verdict, he looked a little surly, like he'd just been through a wringer. When the trial started, Owen had pegged him as the foreman considering his overbearing need to control the conversation during voir dire, but so far, she'd been wrong about every single aspect of this case.

The judge dismissed the jury and then the defendant. Ben turned to her. "I'm going back to talk to them. Want to join me?"

Talking to the jury after the verdict could be a mixed bag, especially if you'd lost the case, but when she trained new prosecutors, Owen had always emphasized trying to do so since the jurors' feedback about what worked and what didn't could be a valuable learning tool. Of course, before now her visits to the jury room had always consisted of a session of praise for her presentation of the case and confirmation that she'd been on the right side of the law. Hard to imagine this jury would have anything to say that made sense. She considered sending Ben on his own, but maybe she needed to hear for herself why they had taken a simple fact pattern and twisted it into knots.

The jurors were clutching their coats and their bags, and the big guy, juror eighteen, had already bolted when the attorneys entered the room. Defense counsel, Tom Moss, shook each juror's hand and personally thanked them for doing the right thing by his client. Owen ducked her head to hide her distaste and wondered if he would celebrate by smoking a bowl of his rumored stash. When she looked back up, Summer was staring at her with a knowing smile. *Why do I feel like she knows everything I'm thinking?*

"Lots of doubt," juror seven said to Moss. "Way reasonable."

Owen wanted to roll her eyes. "Would it give any of you pause if you knew he'd been arrested for possession of marijuana before?" She'd blurted out the words and immediately wanted to reel them back in. First rule of interacting with the jury—do not shame them, especially with information they couldn't, wouldn't, know when they'd decided the case. She hadn't been allowed to bring up the prior arrest during the guilt-innocence phase of the trial because it wasn't considered relevant to the facts of this case. She'd been hoping the judge would allow them to broach the subject during punishment, but even that was iffy considering the first case had been dismissed after Jex successfully completed probation.

"I don't know," juror five said. "I do know Summer was a great foreperson. She forced us to look hard at the evidence, especially the part about how your client didn't own the car and whether the marijuana was where he could get to it easily."

Damn. She shook her head as she listened to the jurors tell Moss what a great job he'd done balancing out the story the police officer had relayed, and she felt foolish for all the extra effort she'd expended connecting with Summer during the trial with pointed looks and smiles only to find Summer had convinced the jurors to vote for the other side. Juror eighteen had had the right idea about bolting. She should've never come back to talk to these people, no matter how alluring this one might be. She waved to the jurors and mumbled something about having to be in another court and walked toward the door. She was in the well of the courtroom when she heard a voice call her name.

"Owen, sorry, Ms. Lassiter, may I speak with you for a moment?"

Owen turned slowly, hoping she wouldn't regret the interaction. "Yes?"

"I know you were disappointed in the verdict. Losing isn't your thing, is it?"

Owen glanced around, but there was no one else in the room. Still, she lowered her voice. "I don't think this is an appropriate conversation."

"He didn't know the marijuana was there."

Summer's voice was firm, like a teacher telling a student their answer was dead wrong. Owen wasn't sure what reaction Summer was trying to provoke, but she was steaming in response. "You have no way of knowing that for sure. You don't know what the defendant really knew, only the self-serving statements he made in court. Your job was to stick to the facts, and the facts are he had marijuana in his possession. Any other jury would've taken less than an hour to come to the conclusion he'd violated the law, and I'm mystified why you could not do the same."

Summer nodded in response, but more like a patronizing pat on the head than an acknowledgment that she was correct, and Owen instantly regretted the outburst. Everything about this day, from losing the case to losing her temper, was completely out of character for her. Her best bet was to call it a day. So why was she reluctant to walk away from Summer even when she was unable to get past her anger?

CHAPTER THREE

Summer stared at Owen trying to see past her words, but the walls she had in place were tall and thick, and it was pretty clear she wasn't used to being challenged. Summer considered ways to convince her that she wasn't challenging her adversarial skills, but she couldn't come up with anything to say that wouldn't reveal the core of the matter—that her doubt about whether Jex was guilty wasn't simply reasonable, it was absolute. Unfortunately, Owen probably wouldn't deem the source of her certainty to be credible. Hell, the idea she could hear voices and see outcomes didn't resonate with many people after what had happened in Santa Cruz, giving her little reason to think things would be different here where no one had any positive experience with her special skills. And that was the point, right? She'd moved here with Faith to start a new life. One where she worked nine-to-five and work life didn't bubble over into her dreams. She should start that new life now by ignoring Owen's baiting and leaving this place.

She tamped down her draw to Owen's allure and simply said, "I'm sorry you don't agree with the verdict. Our decision was unanimous, and I don't have anything else to say about it."

"Well, that's really helpful."

Summer could swear there was a trace of wistfulness underneath the sarcasm in Owen's tone. She got it. Owen, like everyone else, had a facade they showed to the rest of the world to accomplish what she needed to get done. Her instinct was to tell Owen everything—what she'd seen, what she knew in her soul, even if it didn't align with the evidence presented in court, but she had a facade of her own and it didn't allow for slips. She thought of Faith, starting fresh at a new school where no one had preconceived notions about her odd mother who had visions and heard voices, and her decision was made. "I'm sorry."

She reached out a hand to soften the blow and was surprised when Owen accepted the gesture. For the second she clasped Owen's hand, she felt defeat and the burden that came with it—the power of the feeling completely out of proportion with the gravity of the case they'd just heard. Owen was a deep well, and she needed to walk away or risk drowning in her depths.

The elevator banks weren't as full as they had been that morning, but Summer bypassed them for the escalator, not wanting to deal with the onslaught of emotions that would come from the crushing closeness of so many people. On the ride down, she looked around. The courthouse here in Dallas was over twice the size of the one in Santa Cruz, and much less personal, but being here dredged up good memories as well as bad. She could hear the echo of her grandmother's words. She'd helped many people, but it wasn't her duty to make them listen. She'd done her part and it was time to move on. A new place, a new life—not just for Faith—but for her as well. She stepped off the escalator and faced the large, looming doors, ready to be on the other side of them.

"Excuse me, miss."

She turned and stared at the stranger who'd brushed against her and the floor shifted, tilting her out of balance. She opened her mouth to say something but promptly shut it again because the word that formed—DANGER—made no sense. He was short, shorter than her, and slim. She could take him in a pinch, but what she could physically see didn't signal she'd need to. Deep blue eyes, close-cropped blond hair, and a kind smile—nothing to signal danger. Even the hint of a scar above his left eye looked like the kind you'd get doing normal things like falling off a bike, but everything she couldn't see rumbled beneath the surface like a dangerous volcano.

"Are you okay?" the stranger asked and reached for her arm.

Summer edged away, unnerved by her own impoliteness. "Yes," she said, desperately trying to calm her breath. "I'm fine."

He held a piece of paper toward her. "Do you know where the 282nd court is?"

Summer summoned the wherewithal to point toward the security guards manning the entrance to the building. "They'll know."

"Thank you."

His smile was warm and kind. Nothing to indicate he was ominous in any way, but Summer was desperate to escape his presence nevertheless. She nodded and rushed out the door, determined that once she left this place, she would never return.

An hour later, she pulled up in front of Faith's school and waved to her daughter, who was standing outside, apart from the other kids, feigning nonchalance. Faith tossed her backpack in the rear seat and climbed into the passenger side. Summer took a deep breath and squelched the tumble of feelings she'd had from the courthouse to focus on her daughter, whose energy was a mix of adrenaline and anxiety. "How'd it go today?"

"Fine."

"Now see, in my world, 'fine' means not fine. Like really not fine. How not fine was it?"

"I don't want to talk about it."

Summer wanted to push or, short of getting Faith to open up, intuit what she could, but she'd resisted both. Tuning her out was hard, but hearing every random thought of a girl on the cusp of being a teenager was harder. Besides, Faith had always come to her when she needed help, and she had to trust that she would this time. New beginnings in strange places came with all sorts of baggage. Hell, she was having trouble adjusting, making it completely unrealistic to expect Faith would fit right in. She wasn't going to solve Faith's problems by being a prying, helicopter mom, but she did have another idea. "I'm on board with the no talking, but I finished up jury duty today and I think we should celebrate. How about we pick up Nan and go out to eat?"

"Yes!" Faith fist-pumped the air. "Can I pick the place?"

"Too late," Summer said. "I have an incredible craving for Thai food." The craving had started moments before she left the courthouse. Letters floated in the air in front of her, and she struggled to keep her eyes on the road. "How about Simply Thai? It's downtown. I think."

"Thai is great."

Summer grinned. "A daughter after my heart. We haven't had good Thai food in months."

"Yep. It's been a steady stream of Nan's top ten funeral casseroles since we moved in."

Faith's comment had no tone, but Summer felt a pang of guilt nevertheless. For uprooting their little family, for disrupting her grandmother's quiet life, for not having the means to take care of her daughter on her own. "We won't always have to be so careful. It's just with the move and all… I'll find steady work soon."

Faith drummed her fingers on the console. "It's cool. So you wanna tell me about jury duty or save it for dinner?"

"It was pretty cut-and-dry," Summer said. "We found the defendant not guilty." Summer immediately flashed to Owen's heated stare as she read the verdict in the courtroom and then again when the attorneys had come back to the jury room to talk to them. She'd felt the sear of Owen's annoyance burning into her skin long after she was out of Owen's presence. She'd made her mad. She got it, but there wasn't anything she could do about it. Owen's case had holes, and she might be used to other people glossing over that, but Summer wasn't that person. The whole experience had worn her out, and she was grateful her only connection to the criminal justice system in Dallas was the short-lived stint on the jury. No matter how intriguing and nice to look at Owen Lassiter might be.

"You sure there wasn't more to it?" Faith asked.

Summer shrugged to disguise her surprise at Faith's insight. "Nope." She wasn't lying. Not entirely. There wasn't more to it. At least not anything she could put into words. The heavy onslaught of feelings she'd experienced at the courthouse was likely more about past baggage than any future portent. "I did get paid a whopping twelve dollars for my time. Check's in the mail."

"Remind me not to order any appetizers at dinner."

"Or dessert," Summer said with a faux serious expression. "Seriously, though, maybe we should try that new frozen custard place after dinner. I ate creepy cafeteria food for lunch and I could use a treat."

"Welcome to my world." Faith sighed dramatically.

"Today, the only edible thing in the cafeteria line was an apple. I'm starving."

"You know, Nan would be happy to pack a lunch for you."

"Uh, have you met her? I'm not sure how your side of the family lived to procreate. I love her, but she's not so good with the cooking. I have enough problems being the new girl without unwrapping a sack of surprise entrees in the cafeteria. I'll take my chances with the mystery meat everyone else is eating, thank you very much."

Summer's heart broke a little at the mention of problems, and her stomach clenched with the memory of the issues she'd faced back when she was Faith's age. She wanted to press Faith for details, take action, but she knew it wasn't that simple, and any action on her part was bound to make things worse. The best thing she could do was to be available to listen if Faith decided she wanted to talk.

A couple of hours later, they were back in the car, this time with Nan riding shotgun. "What's this place we're going to for dinner?" Nan asked.

"Mom picked it out," Faith said. "How did you hear about it, Mom?"

"Around," Summer said, not wanting to admit she'd pulled the name out of the ether as she was leaving the courthouse. She thought back to the jury room with the stack of to-go menus—something Faith would've mocked for being so last century—trying to remember if this place had been one of those, but she didn't think it was. Yet, she'd known from the moment she left the courthouse that she needed to go to this place, and she needed to go there soon. Please let the food be good or else Faith and Nan were never going to let her live down the choice.

The front of the restaurant was marked by a bright red

awning and red doors. "Simply Thai" was painted in elegant script across the doors, and everything about the curb appeal was welcoming and open, but as she drove past, looking for a place to park, Summer gripped the steering wheel, tensed and anxious at the prospect of approaching this place, welcoming ambiance to the contrary.

"Mom, are you okay?"

Summer looked in the rearview mirror and saw Faith staring back at her, her eyes scrunched with concern which she quickly sought to allay. "Sure, why?"

"Well, for one thing, you're gripping the steering wheel like you're scared it's going to fly off, and for another, if you want that parking spot, I suggest you turn into it before the line of cars behind us starts honking."

Summer smiled to hide the fact she'd lost track of where they were for a moment and steered the car into the space. When she turned the car off, Nan's hand reached out to grab hers.

"You okay?"

Summer pulled the keys from the ignition and jingled them in the air. "I'm great other than the fact I'm starving. Let's order all the things and eat until we can't move. What say you?"

"I vote yes," Faith said, tugging at the door handle to display her exuberance.

"Who am I to stand in the way?" Nan asked with a shrug, her eyes tracking Summer as she stowed her keys in her purse, clearly not convinced there was nothing going on.

"Later," Summer whispered. She shot a look at Faith, who was already out of the car. "I promise."

Nan humphed. "Fine. Dinner is a stress free zone."

Two minutes later, Nan's words floated through Summer's head as she stepped up on the curb toward the door of Simply

Thai. Stress free would be nice. The move to Dallas had been fraught with complications from the logistics of moving their belongings to the stress of trying to find a job with what had to be one of the most unconventional résumés around. Not as unconventional as, say, astronaut or magician, but once people started asking for specifics about what exactly a consultant for the district attorney's office actually did, she tended to falter. Maybe she needed to spend some time coming up with a better script for her job interviews. One that didn't leave her mumbling something about evidence and witnesses and jury prep in rambling sentences that didn't actually piece together.

She glanced around, but the door to the restaurant was no longer in view. She could've sworn it was only a few steps from the curb, but all she could make out now were concrete stairs leading to the back door of another building. The building didn't have a sign, but it looked like the rear entrance of a store or club. The air around her became gray as if the sun has suddenly set and the streetlights hadn't gotten the message. She searched through the haze for some clue about what she was supposed to see, hear, do, but all she heard were the hard footfalls of someone running, and the sound was fading into the distance.

"Mom?"

She shook her head, but the fog was gone. The sidewalk was back beneath her feet, and the door to the restaurant looked as inviting as it had when they'd pulled up here moments ago. Something had happened here, would happen here—she didn't have a clue what, but it wasn't good and it wasn't specific enough for her to do a damn thing about it. She touched a hand to her head and focused on Faith. "Sorry, I'm a little faint, but it's probably due to the crappy cafeteria food from lunch."

Faith grabbed her hand and tugged her toward the door. "Let's cure that with a big bunch of super-spicy food."

The restaurant was packed, typical Friday night in Dallas, but miraculously, they managed to slip in just as another family was leaving. Summer watched Faith's gaze linger on the mom, dad, and two kids exiting the restaurant, and she wondered if Faith ever longed for the typical family structure or if she was okay with just the two of them. Three now that Nan was a regular fixture. If she concentrated really hard, she might get the answer, but she'd tried really hard to cultivate headspace where Faith could think her own thoughts without worrying her mom was monitoring them. She'd gotten so good at tuning out Faith's feelings, she sometimes sensed a distance between them she regretted, but not more than giving her daughter the gift of privacy.

They followed the hostess to the back of the restaurant, a crappy section, but Summer was relieved to be tucked away from the rest of the crowd. They slid into the booth and began perusing the menu.

Faith immediately began pointing out her favorite dishes. "What do you like, Nan?"

"I have no idea. This is my first foray into the land of Thai food, but everything sounds wonderful. How about we have a little bit of everything? And dinner's on me," she said, punctuating her remark with a hard glare in Summer's direction.

Summer recognized the look as one meant to deter all detractors, but for some reason she couldn't articulate, it was important that she take care of the tab. "Not tonight," she said. "You've done enough for us. The least I can do is introduce you to the wonder and spice of Thailand. You're going to love it."

"Anything will be better than the endless casseroles," Nan replied. "I appreciate that everyone loved my Charlie, but he's not having to eat the damn things."

"I thought you loved the casseroles," Faith said. "I mean, you do serve them pretty regularly."

"Faith," Summer said, shaking her head and wondering when exactly kids started developing filters.

"Not," Nan said. "But the damn things kept coming, even weeks after the funeral, and I couldn't bear throwing them away, so they piled up in the freezer. I'm tired of them too, but since I can't cook worth a damn and your mom's too busy looking for a job, they've kept us alive. Am I right?"

"How about we share the load?" Summer said. "You two can each get a night, we'll go out to eat one night, and I'll cook the rest of the time? I need to start pulling my weight, especially since I can't seem to find a permanent job and the temp company wasn't very patient with the fact I couldn't show up today because of jury duty."

"Deal, but you don't have to feel bad about working hard to find a new start." Nan patted her hand. "I know I seem crochety a lot of the time, but I'm really happy to have you both here. Charlie's death left a big hole. It's not the same talking to him when he's not here in person."

"Does he talk to you, Nan?" Faith asked.

"Well…"

Nan glanced at Summer and Summer nodded. It was inevitable that Faith would have questions like this, considering she was already starting to see signs that Faith had the same gift she shared with Nan. Not for the first time, Summer wondered if her mother also had the ability to hear the dead and read people's thoughts and had simply chosen to hide it or ignore it. Lord knows she'd never used it to try to improve their relationship. Her mother had never been receptive to talking about what it meant when Summer started having visions and hearing other people's thoughts at the tender age of ten. Summer never wanted Faith to feel as adrift as she had, confused and scared by the friends she couldn't see but who constantly occupied her thoughts. That was part of the reason, when she'd decided she needed to leave Santa Cruz, she accepted Nan's generous offer of hospitality. Landlocked Dallas was no comparison to seaside Santa Cruz, but there was no substitute for family who loved and accepted you for who you were.

"Charlie does talk to me," Nan said. "He even gives me recipes he says I should try to make for you all, but I suppose being dead has affected his memory of my disasters in the kitchen."

"I thought I saw him one night last week," Faith said. "When I went to get a glass of water." She giggled. "He was wearing an apron."

Nan laughed with her. "I know exactly the one. I'll show it to you when we get home. I'll even give it to you if you learn to cook. Get your mom to teach you—she definitely got your grandfather's cooking gene."

Faith started scrolling through her phone. "Looking up chicken tikka masala recipes, right now. Can't wait."

Summer watched the exchange between her daughter and her grandmother, and their easy camaraderie cemented her decision to stick around for a while. She hadn't found a job yet, and she'd already pissed off the most beautiful woman she'd met, but she'd find a way to make a home here because family was important, living and dead, and she wanted her daughter to appreciate everything she had.

Chapter Four

Owen tossed her partially eaten sandwich on the desk and sighed.

"If you're not going to eat that, give it here," Mary said, snapping her fingers.

"It's not any good. The chicken salad has grapes in it and they're past their prime."

"You say that like I'll care." Mary patted her stomach. "Good is relative when you're eating for two. I feel like everything I ingest is immediately going to feed Mr. X."

"If you keep calling your unborn child Mr. X, he's going to have way bigger problems than fighting you for food."

"Whatever. Don't get me wrong, I'm very excited about having a family, but I know that once Mr. X leaves the comfort of the womb for the real world, the rest of my life, and my sandwiches, will not be my own. In the meantime, I'll take whatever I can get, especially if you're going to freely toss me your leftovers."

Owen dutifully handed her the sandwich. "I guess I'm just not hungry."

Mary bit into the sandwich and moaned. "This is perfection." She wiped her lips with a napkin. "I know what your problem is. You're still sulking."

"I don't know what you're talking about." Owen mustered all the sincerity she could find, but she knew her declaration fell flat.

"Liar. You lost one case. A tiny little drug possession case, marijuana—not even real drugs. And the case wasn't even technically yours. You've had all weekend to put it behind you, but you're still obsessing over it. Most of us lost a dozen misdemeanor cases before we hit our second year. Sorry not sorry you're just now making it into the club, but seriously, O, the moping has got to go."

Owen leaned back in her chair and stared at the ceiling. Her annoyance was legit, but she knew Mary and everyone else was tired of dealing with the fallout of her recent loss, and she needed to shake her malaise, but she kept coming back to one central issue. "I really thought we had a connection. If I could be that wrong about my take on her, then what's to say I'm not going to mess up jury selection in this case?"

"Oh, you're back to obsessing over the pretty blond forewoman." Mary poked the last piece of sandwich in her mouth and gave a tiny moan as if she were eating her way through a tasting menu from a Michelin star restaurant. "Do you still have her questionnaire? Why don't you just track her down and ask her out already? Clearly, you're not going to get over this until you get her out of your system."

"Hush your mouth. I don't want to go out with her."

"Short of jumping in a time machine, that's probably all your obsession is going to get you. It's not like you can convince her to change her mind on the verdict now, but you could get laid provided you can be more charming out of the courtroom than in it. Your charges will thank me if you do. You've been really uptight lately."

Had she? She'd been focused for sure. Her recent reassignment to the Adams case was an enormous responsibility, but she'd prepared for a case this big her entire career. And with a reliable eyewitness, a guilty verdict was practically guaranteed. So why did she have a nagging feeling something was off? Was her uncertainty tied to the loss last week or was there a problem with their evidence in the case she wasn't seeing yet—one waiting to explode at the worst possible moment?

"Let it rest, Mare. That isn't the kind of connection I'm talking about and you know it." Owen felt the burn of a blush at Mary's raised eyebrows. She knew her all too well. "Even if it was, I don't have time for a love life right now. I'm relying on you to help me focus."

"We have very different ideas about how to focus." Mary pointed at her belly. "But of course, my methods can be distracting in the long run. Fine, let's talk about the case. Something's on your mind. Spill."

Owen stared at the board they'd erected in the war room, trying to figure out how to put into words the gut churning she'd experienced since she'd done a deep dive into the evidence. She pointed at the indictment which was posted smack in the middle. "Maybe I'm uptight because something's not adding up. I can't put my finger on it, but we're missing something."

"That's nice and vague. Any chance you could come up with something a little more specific?"

She could, but saying the words out loud would make it real and she wasn't sure she wanted to go there. Yet. County Commissioner Keith Adams was not only one of the most powerful men in Dallas County, he was one of the most beloved. The one poor soul who'd taken him on in the last election cycle had only managed to garner eight percent of the vote, and considering the low turnout of the off-season election, the opponent's votes had likely come from his own friends and family. Adams was universally liked, and after his wife had been murdered, his favorability ratings had grown exponentially. To most everyone in the county, he could do no wrong. Everyone but her.

Since the first time she'd met Adams at a party fundraiser she'd attended in support of her boss, Owen had a nagging feeling there was more to his down-home, hail-fellow-well-met routine than met the eye, but she had absolutely no evidence to back up the instinct. And for a person who relied on evidence in everything she did, the absence of it meant she couldn't, wouldn't, voice her concern in public. But Mary wasn't public. She was the closest thing Owen had to a best friend, and who better to try out her half-baked theory?

Owen walked to the door and glanced outside to make sure no one was standing nearby and quietly pulled it to. When she turned back, Mary was rolling her palm in the air, signaling her impatience with the wait. Owen took a deep breath and expelled her theory like she was struggling for air. "What if Commissioner Adams was behind the murder? What if he hired Fuentes to do it? To make it look like a burglary gone wrong?"

"Wow. I thought you were going to say something like you didn't like what you had for lunch. I had no idea you were going to try to tank our case."

Owen stared at Mary. She sat with her arms crossed, rolling her eyes like she wasn't remotely buying into her theory. She should shut up now, dial back what she could, and get back to work preparing to use the evidence they did have to prosecute the only true suspect in the case. But she couldn't. The floodgates had opened, and she had to let all the water out or she would drown in the sea of doubt.

"Hear me out." Owen paced the room, conscious she was waving her arms as she talked, but needing the motion to expel the energy that came with dumping the contents of her brain out on the table. "DPD didn't even consider him as a suspect. You don't think Fuentes's attorney isn't going to bring that up? It's basic criminal investigation. Look at the people closest to the victim, spouses especially."

Mary held up her palm. "I'll hear you out, but first I need you to take a seat. You're making me crane my neck to see you, and the constant motion is making me nauseous."

Owen paused to assess if Mary was being patronizing and decided her request was sincere. She slid into the nearest chair but stayed on the edge of her seat, certain the need to spring into action might come at any moment.

"Okay, much better," Mary said. She reached for a folder on the desk. "We have the interview notes for the cops who showed up first at the scene. I assume you have them memorized?"

It was Owen's well-known quirk—the ability to read and instantly memorize information—that had gotten her through many a tough spot from college to career, but while the talent was helpful, it could also be frustrating in that she never forgot what she'd seen or read, so when things didn't add up, the inconsistency might nag at her for days. Here, she hoped, the skill would simply make it easier to make her argument. "Yes, I do. Adams received a call from his maid at ten o'clock on Saturday evening. He'd been at a restaurant with Mayor Heller and was on his way home when he got a call from the maid, who'd dropped by the house because she'd accidentally left her wallet at the house. She found the back door standing open and Mrs. Adams's dead body in the living room."

"Did anyone else live in the house besides the commissioner and his wife?"

"No. I mean, technically, their daughter, Ashley, lives there, but she's away at college."

"Okay." Mary drew out the word a bit.

"Okay what?"

"Are you ready for me to start poking holes in your theory now, or do you want me to wait until the end?"

Owen swallowed a sharp retort. She knew she sounded a bit like one of those conspiracist types who hung out in Dealey Plaza every November, ready and willing to tell tourists their theory of how Lee Harvey didn't act alone and why. "I'll take my dose of Mary smackdown when I'm done."

She went through the list of facts, highlighting several in particular: the security system wasn't on, nothing was taken, and so far, no one had turned up a motive for the killing. "Okay, now it's your turn," Owen said. "Convince me I'm wrong."

Mary raised her hands. "I'm not saying you're wrong. These are all good points to raise, but I do have counterpoints to make. First off, Adams wasn't home when the burglary occurred. He had no idea the maid was going to come by, and if she hadn't, presumably, he would've arrived home to find his dead wife and had to call the police, thereby incurring suspicion about whether he'd simply murdered her and then acted like he'd just arrived home. A smart person who'd arranged to have his wife killed probably would've had a better plan for how and when her dead body would be discovered. Don't you think?"

"You have a point, but it's based on some critical assumptions. For instance, the planning part. Commissioner Adams would likely think he could talk his way out of anything that involved the police, one-on-one."

"I suppose. As for the security system, Adams told the police there had been problems with the system recently. The company's reports back this up."

Owen wanted to point out that the security system's failure could have been plotted in advance as well but realized again she sounded like the kind of conspiracy theorist that as a prosecutor she tried her best to avoid. Still, she couldn't deny the nagging feeling the police hadn't focused on Adams the way they would a spouse who wasn't an important city official. "Fine, but don't you think it's odd there's no evidence of any crime other than the assault? Nothing was taken, she wasn't raped. Fuentes has priors, but in those cases, he broke into homes and actually stole something. There's no evidence he even tried to remove any property from Adams's house. Seriously, why did he choose that particular house to break into?"

"She surprised him before he could take anything?"

"And his reaction was to shoot her? A guy with no history of violence against another person breaks into a house to take stuff and encounters the homeowner. Instead of turning tail to get the hell out, he pulls out a gun and shoots her not once, but three times?" Owen shook her head. "It's hard for me to swallow."

"I get it," Mary said, "But you're violating the first rule of investigations—the simplest explanation is usually the right one. The case is high-bitched because it's Fuentes's third offense. You think he didn't know that was a possibility? He reacted in a way that seemed rational at the time even if it doesn't pan out in the light of day. If all criminals were rational, you and I would be out of work really fast."

She was right and Owen knew it, but Mary's rationale didn't do anything to quell the unease she felt about this case, and she wondered again if she'd be better off if Ron had stayed on, leaving her free from the repercussions of trying a case about which she had doubts. But she'd vied for the opportunity and now that she had it, she would step up and do everything she could to put Mrs. Adams's killer behind bars.

"Point taken, but I want to go through everything again. In detail, like we've never seen it before. I'll clear the rest of the week. Let's set up meetings with the responding officers, Detectives Lacey and Garcia, and the witness who saw Fuentes leaving the house."

"Deal. I've got a doctor appointment on Thursday afternoon—nothing major—just a checkup, but otherwise I'm in for whatever. I'll get Kira to round up the witness and the officers and get them scheduled in," she said, referring to their investigator.

"Perfect." Owen's phone buzzed to signal an incoming text and she checked the screen. "Gotta go. One of the children needs some help." She knew she shouldn't refer to the misdemeanor court attorneys as children, but she couldn't help it since they often acted like they'd never been through law school. Had she been as clueless when she was first starting out? God, she hoped not.

"Go. Solve the world's problems. I'll get these interviews set up and text you the schedule."

Owen strode to the door, confident Mary would handle things and relieved to have her on the case. Now, she needed to shrug off all thoughts of last week's loss and Summer Byrne and focus on winning the biggest case of her career.

❖

Hands tightening. Fingers pressing hard. Gasping for air. Kicking hard. The hands had to be connected to a body. Hurt it and it will release its grasp. Have to break free. Vision fading. Darkness. Falling.

Summer jerked awake and reached for her throat, half expecting to find fingers threaded around her neck, but there was only her own skin, unencumbered. She sat up on the couch and took deep gulps of air, vowing never to take the ability to breathe for granted, while she reached for her phone. Without even looking, she started punching in the numbers, stopping short before abandoning the errand and dropping the phone to the couch cushion. She'd repeated the same ritual every day for the past week, never completing the call and suffering a pang of guilt each time she disconnected the phone that intensified the next time she had the dream. For all she knew, the violence in her dream was a past event—nothing she could prevent. But the dread loomed and there had to be a reason someone, somewhere was showing her these images. If not to prevent harm, then why? The upshot of her indecision was a shattered sleep schedule and a dark mood that had been noticed by both Faith and Nan, who carried on whispered conversations about what was up with her since she'd been on jury duty. If only the bad dreams had had something to do with jury duty instead of the violent attack on a man she'd never met. If she was going to dream about jury duty, she'd prefer to imagine the appearance of Owen Lassiter, the stubborn, steamy prosecutor who gave off boatloads of mysterious vibes. What would Owen have to say about her dreams? She had a feeling she knew.

"Another dream?"

Damn. Summer looked across the room at Nan, who was standing in the doorway between the living room and the kitchen, a knowing smile on her face. There really wasn't any point in lying, as much as she wanted to deny the dream and avoid the conversation that was about to happen. But seeing the future didn't necessarily mean she knew how to avoid it. Her entire life had upended on that point alone. Might as well get it over with. "Yes."

"Might do you some good to talk about it." Nan walked into the room, and for the first time Summer noticed she carried a tray full of sandwiches, cut into cute little diagonals. "I made you lunch, and I promise it's edible. Hard for even me to ruin a sandwich. You haven't been eating…"

Her last words formed a complete sentence, but Summer knew Nan wanted to add "since the day after you finished jury duty." She might have been able to convince Faith that the little episode she'd had outside of Simply Thai was a consequence of exhaustion, but Nan wasn't buying it. Maybe it would make her feel better to talk to Nan about it. Get her advice about what to do. She reached for a piece of sandwich and held it up for examination. "Pimento cheese. Yum." She bit into the soft white bread and moaned when the tangy cheese mixture hit her taste buds and finished out with a surprise kick of heat. "Jalapeños?"

"Yep. I'm mixing it up in my old age. It's store-bought, but delicious. You like?"

"Love." Summer devoured the rest of the sandwich point and reached for another. "Never, ever have it any other way."

Nan set the platter on the coffee table and settled into the recliner across from the couch. Everything in the room was classic seventies and Summer loved the comfort of the gold tones. She pulled the crotched afghan over her bare feet and contemplated another piece of pimento cheese sandwich.

"You'll feel better when you share what's on your mind," Nan said. "I promise the sandwiches will still be there when you're done talking."

"Stop it."

"What?"

"Stop reading my thoughts. It's not polite."

"Your mother teach you that? Sounds like something she would say."

It was exactly what her mother would—had—said every time Summer would point out that her actions didn't match her thoughts or vice versa. For a long time, before she'd found Nan, she'd learned to hide her gift to keep from displeasing her mother, who either didn't have the ability to see and hear what was invisible and unspoken or didn't view it as a gift if she did. "She might have had a point, you know. It's not good to have your every thought be examined by someone else. It can stunt a person."

"Bullshit. If more people stopped living in their heads, the world might be a better place," Nan said. "Secrets, lack of communication—these are the things that contribute to misunderstandings, manipulations, mayhem. Get it all out in the open, I say."

Summer shook her head. She was used to Nan's rants, but usually they were directed at the world in general and this one felt pretty personal. "What do you know about what I'm thinking?"

"I'm not reading your mind, dear. Not on purpose, anyway, but I can tell something is bothering you. Something heavy. You're scared, both about the thing and about telling someone about it. Why not tell me as kind of a test run? See how it goes and then you can decide what else to do about it."

She had a point. Summer wasn't convinced Nan's motives weren't totally voyeuristic—she did love a good bit of drama—but it might do her good to try speaking out loud the dream and seeing if, in the light of day, it had an impact on someone besides just her. "When we went to Simply Thai last week, I felt something ominous outside. Something bad happened and the person who did it ran away. Since then, I've been having dreams about a man I spoke to at the courthouse for all of thirty seconds. I keep seeing him mugged, strangled. I can feel the loss of breath, the bones of his neck breaking. He falls to the ground and is gasping for air, but his windpipe is crushed and he can't breathe. I'm not entirely certain, but it feels like it's happening near the restaurant, and you know, the name of the restaurant popped in my head right after I ran into this guy." She shook her head. "I'd never even heard of the place before, and I got an ominous feeling when we were standing outside."

"Pretty intense. Did you see anything else?"

"Not that I can remember. I've dreamed the exact same scenario every time I've fallen asleep since and it doesn't change."

"Any markers?"

Summer smiled, strangely comforted by the familiar term. Now this was the thing Summer liked about talking to Nan. They spoke the same language, probably because Nan had been the one to guide her the very few first times she'd had a dream that turned out to be real. "I can make out the sign for the restaurant and I catch a glimpse of the parking lot across the street, but nothing to indicate date or time."

"Hmm." Nan took one of the sandwiches and nibbled around the edge. "I don't suppose you've googled to see if it's already happened."

"Done and no. There have been a rash of muggings downtown, but none of the victims are my guy. I may not have picked up many markers, but I know exactly what he looks like. He has a scar." She pointed at her forehead. "Right above his left eyebrow. It's faint, but slightly jagged. Like he let it heal on its own, without any stitches."

"How about the mugger? Did you get a good look at him?"

Summer shrugged. "Not great. He's tall, lanky, but he was wearing a mask."

"What do you want to do?"

"I want to forget I saw anything. You think that's possible?"

Nan hunched her shoulders in an unconvincing way. "I guess if you want to keep having the dreams you can do whatever you want. Sleep is underrated, in my opinion."

Summer considered chunking a sandwich at her but decided against it. "I think I need to make a call."

"You'll feel better when you do."

"No one knows me here. I mean really *knows me*. I'd like to keep it that way."

Nan regarded her with a sage expression. "You're calling in a tip. It's no different from the many crackpots who do the same, but you have real information. Valuable information."

"Allegedly. I don't have a name, a time, or a place." Summer closed her eyes and ran through every detail of the scene for the thousandth time, searching for any clues about when the mugging had or would occur, but like every other time, she came up empty, an accurate match for the way she felt knowing something might happen she wouldn't be able to prevent.

"What would you tell Faith to do?"

The question kicked Summer in the gut. "Not fair. Not fair at all."

"And yet, you know deep down you would tell Faith to do whatever she had to do to try to prevent someone from being hurt. Am I right?"

She was, but Summer didn't want to admit it. She'd spent the last few years working with the district attorney's office in Santa Cruz using her powers to channel the truth in a series of criminal cases. The work was fulfilling and she embraced the tension and uncertainty that had come with every new revelation, every obligation to share with law enforcement the contents of her dreams, but she knew too well how fallible her visions could be, especially when, like now, they were incredibly vague as to time and date. If the universe really wanted her to prevent something bad from happening, you'd think it would be more interested in providing better intel.

"Fine, I'm calling." She picked up her phone and looked up the number for the local precinct. She glanced at Nan and took comfort from her reassuring nod. When the voice on the other line answered, she forced a confidence she did not feel. "I'd like to report a crime."

Chapter Five

Owen shot awake at the loud noise, but still impaired by the haze of the deep sleep she'd been rousted from, she was unable to make out the source until she spotted the light flashing from her phone on the nightstand. She grabbed it and squinted to make out the number on the screen. Unknown. Her gut clenched and she answered the call. "Lassiter."

"Owen, it's Kira. We've got a problem."

"Hang on." Owen noted the time—three a.m.—set the phone back on the nightstand, and climbed out of bed. Kira's ominous tone told her she needed to be a helluva lot more awake than she was right now if she wanted to process whatever news was headed her way. She padded to the bathroom and splashed cold water on her face and stared at her reflection in the mirror. She looked like shit, even for someone rousted from bed in the middle of the night. Dark circles under her eyes, and she was desperately in need of a haircut. She brushed an errant curl off her face and trudged back to the phone, dreading whatever prompted this middle of the night alarm.

"Talk to me. What's up?"

"Leo Joule was mugged tonight. Last I heard, he was

unconscious. The responding officer recognized his name and called to let me know they took him to Parkland. I'm on my way there now."

Owen was instantly wide-awake. "I'll meet you there."

"I'm not far from you if you want me to swing by and pick you up."

There wasn't a trace of anything other than professionalism in Kira's tone, but Owen felt uncomfortable at Kira's words, remembering why Kira knew exactly where she lived. They'd only been together a couple of times. They'd had fun and they'd both agreed that was all it would ever be, no matter how many times they repeated it. Owen suspected if she ever wanted more, Kira would probably be game, but she'd avoided going there and she had no intention of changing. She should drive herself tonight, but it was silly to pass up the opportunity to talk to her investigator about what it meant that their star witness had been injured. "Thanks. I'll meet you downstairs."

Owen strode to her closet and slid several hangers aside until she found the tan suit she liked to wear when she was meeting with witnesses who needed to be put at ease. She paired it with a chocolate brown shirt and hurriedly dressed while her mind whirred with questions. Leo Joule was the only eyewitness who'd seen Fuentes at the house the night Mrs. Adams had been killed. He hadn't seen the murder take place, but he'd heard the gunshots and then seen Fuentes running away from the house. Owen had serious doubts about whether he'd actually witnessed both things and in what order, but she couldn't ignore Joule's steadfast determination about how it had gone down. He was the linchpin of their case and had to be protected at all costs.

Kira was waiting in her Dodge muscle car at the curb in front of Owen's building and, not for the first time, she had a comment to make about where Owen lived the minute she stepped into the car.

"The valet tried to get me to move until I flashed my badge. I hope your homeowner dues are worth it. I can't imagine living somewhere where I'd have to wait for some dude in a fancy uniform to fetch my car whenever I wanted to go somewhere."

"You say that now, but when you've worked till midnight and all you want to do is fall into bed, it's pretty sweet to be able to roll up to the front door and toss your keys at the dude, silly uniform or not."

"I can think of better things to spend my county paycheck on."

Owen hid the flicker of annoyance that flared up as Kira needled her, but she couldn't resist a little push back. "Like this car? Seriously, you spend all day driving around in Dallas traffic. When do you ever get to rev this engine and let it fly the way it was intended?"

Kira laughed. "Point taken. I guess we both like having nice things even if we define them differently."

"I guess. Tell me what you know about Joule," she said, glad to have something to talk about besides her wealth. Kira's curiosity about her personal circumstance was one of the main reasons, besides the fact they worked together, that whatever went on between them would never be more serious than a string of one-night stands. If Kira really wanted to know more about her personal life, she could easily use her investigative skills to find out, and Owen often wondered if she had, but was seeking confirmation from the primary source—her—as to what she'd found. But Owen valued her privacy too much to engage in idle banter about her background. Besides her car and her clothes, the high-rise apartment was the only ostensible luxury she indulged in, and if she had it to do over again, she wouldn't have ever invited Kira back to her place and risked rousing her suspicion.

"It happened downtown. Beat cop found him passed out in a parking lot, not six feet from his car. There's a restaurant nearby, but it's closed, and everyone's already gone for the night. We'll get someone out there in the morning to talk to the staff and see if anyone saw anything, and DPD has officers canvassing the area now to see if any of the homeless down there are willing to speak up. Unlikely, but we're doing whatever we can."

"What kind of injuries does he have?"

"That's what's weird. Looks like someone tried to strangle him. No evidence any other weapon was used. Wallet still in his pocket. I guess someone could've scared the perp off while he was in the middle of the holdup, but it seems amateurish to me."

"Or maybe it wasn't a robbery. Maybe someone was sending a message." Owen tapped her fingers against her neck. "Cut off his air to tell him not to talk."

Kira narrowed her eyes. "Seriously? You think Fuentes has the kind of pull to get someone to threaten a witness? I find that highly unlikely."

Owen didn't bother arguing the point. There would be plenty of time to figure out what the evidence meant when they had more evidence to sort through, but she had a nagging suspicion the harm that had come to Joule tonight was not the result of a simple robbery gone wrong. "I want a guard on his room. Someone from the sheriff's department. Around the clock."

"Already in motion. DPD is going to have a fit about that."

Owen knew that was right, but since DPD officers

themselves were witnesses in her case, she didn't want them in the position of guarding her key witness in the event the defense attorney tried to claim Joule's favorable testimony was payback for being protected.

"Here we are," Kira announced, pulling her car right up to the emergency room door. She rolled down her window and flashed her badge at the security guard standing in the drive and he motioned to the parking for the emergency vehicles. "See," she said, "that's respect."

Owen didn't take the bait. She followed Kira into the ER, willing to let her wave her badge around to get them access. She had a badge too, but she preferred to use it only when absolutely necessary rather than advertise her authority. People were generally more willing to reveal things in casual conversation than they were when they thought they were on the record.

A few minutes later, they were in front of a room in the ER guarded by a woman she recognized from the courthouse. She scanned her name badge. "Deputy Franco, how are you doing tonight?"

"Good, Ms. Lassiter, Ms. Vaughn. All quiet so far."

"Is he awake yet?"

"He wasn't a minute ago. The doctor is in with him now." Franco stepped to the side "I'll make sure no one disturbs you if you'd like to talk to him."

Owen nodded and stepped through the door with Kira right behind. Joule and the doctor were the only ones in the room, and to her relief, Joule was awake. He didn't look great, though. "Mr. Joule, I came as soon as I heard."

He looked confused for a moment and the doctor took the opportunity to interject. "I'm Dr. Elias. Are you family?"

Owen felt Kira start to reach for the damn badge again,

and she made a slicing motion with her hand to get her to stop. "No, we've been working together, and I heard from a mutual friend that he's been hurt. Is he okay?"

Dr. Elias glanced at Joule who nodded. "He will be. It's hard to assess the damage to his trachea, but he shouldn't talk for a while. Other than that, he should recover fully."

"That's great news," Owen said, but she filed away the fact that Joule's only significant injury might be to his ability to speak. "May we have a moment alone?"

Dr. Elias studied them both and turned to Joule. "If it's okay with you, but only for a few minutes. You need to rest." He pointed at a pad of paper and pen on the tray next to Joule's bed. "Use that to communicate. I don't want him talking right now. He may be a little confused. He was out for a while. Please do keep your visit short."

Owen waited until the doctor was out of sight and the door closed before launching into her first question. "Did you see who did this to you?"

Joule shook his head immediately. Owen wanted to ask him if he was sure but decided not to press right now. She had a bunch of questions about exactly what had gone down, but she'd let Kira break down all the details, and she nodded in her direction to indicate she should get started.

"I'm sorry to bother you about details when you're probably in pain," Kira said, "But your memory is likely as fresh as it will be right now. Do you have any idea what time you were attacked?"

Joule scrunched his forehead, picked up the pen, and started writing furiously on the pad. As the moments ticked by it became clear he was giving more detail than had been requested. When he finally handed them the pad, she and Kira studied the words.

Just got off work. Bar next to Simply Thai. Would've been

about midnight. Grabbed from behind. Tried to tell him to take my cash but couldn't get the words out. Everything went black and I woke up in the ambulance.

A complete story and it was completely useless. "Did anyone leave the bar with you? Someone who might have seen what happened?"

Joule shook his head.

"Any idea who might have done this?" Kira asked.

Again, with the head shake. This interview was going nowhere, and Owen was getting frustrated. She pulled Kira off to the side. "Contact the bar and the restaurant and see if they have any security cameras that might have caught what happened and seize the footage. If they want a warrant, let me know, but you should be able to get them to comply without one. Interview all of the employees who were working tonight—you know the drill. If you need help, let me know and I'll get Rivera to assign another investigator to help out. I know DPD is going to be doing a lot of the same stuff, but I wanted to hear the unvarnished version. Understood?"

"Absolutely." Kira jerked her chin at Joule, who appeared to be slipping back into sleep. "We done here?"

"I don't think he's got anything useful to add."

"Great, I'll drop you off and get started."

"I can find my own way home."

"Nope, I'm headed that direction anyway."

Back in the car, Kira cleared her throat a few times in a way that Owen recognized as a prelude to an uncomfortable question. "If there's something you want to know, just ask."

"You think this was some kind of warning to Joule—a threat to get him not to testify, don't you?"

"I have no idea," Owen said. "But it seems like there's more to this story than what we see on the surface, so let's start there. You don't think it's odd that he was strangled, that no weapon was used? His wallet was intact, complete with all the cash from his shift. Who mugs a guy with his bare hands and forgets to take the prize? No one, that's who."

"You may be right, but maybe someone interrupted the mugger before he could take anything. That makes this different than all the other muggings that have happened lately."

"Good point. Do what you can to sweet-talk DPD into beefing up the canvass of the neighborhood."

"Will do. We should be able to drum up some leads tomorrow if there's any to be found. You want me to go back and talk to Joule, see if his memory improves?"

"Yes. Tomorrow. I have a hunch he knows something, even if he doesn't remember it."

Kira pulled into the circle drive in front of her building and her car idled. "I could come up. I mean if you want to talk about the case or…"

Owen recognized the offer for what it was, and for a brief moment, she considered taking Kira up on it. Her mind would be whirring about the case for hours, making sleep elusive. Sex might be exactly what she needed to get out of her head and get a decent night's sleep, or what was left of it. But this wasn't some after happy hour interlude. They were both sober and working together on a big case, and Owen didn't need the distraction of giving in to someone who likely felt more than she did when it came to whatever happened between them, especially when she couldn't write off her actions to a drunken indiscretion. She put her hand on the door handle. "I'm pretty beat. Let's talk first thing in the morning."

"Cool."

Kira avoided her eyes, which was fine. Owen didn't need to get caught up in worrying that her investigator was distracted either. She climbed out of the car, nodded to the doorman, and rode the elevator to her apartment. Within moments of entering, she'd hung up her suit and was back in the UT Law T-shirt and plain blue boxers she'd been wearing when Kira had called. She paced the apartment, looking for something out of place she could put right as a symbolic gesture of problem solving, but as usual, everything was in its place, and due to a visit from her housekeeper earlier in the day, it was meticulously clean—exactly the way she liked it.

She settled on a finger of whisky to induce sleep. She poured the Glenmorangie into a short, thick glass and took it with her to bed, where she read her notes about Joule from earlier in the day on her iPad until the words started to swim on the screen. She had no idea how long she'd been asleep when she heard a loud buzzing. *This happened before. How did I make it stop?* She slapped at her nightstand and knocked over something heavy. Finally, she found the switch for her lamp and turned it on. Once her eyes adjusted to the light, she was able to figure out the buzzing was her phone and the something heavy was the whisky glass she'd knocked to the floor. She stared at the phone, surprised it wasn't Kira. She answered. "Lassiter."

"Ms. Lassiter, this is Sergeant Carl Birken down at the Fifth Precinct. Detective Garcia gave me your number. I heard about the witness in the Adams case getting mugged last night."

"Okay." Owen rubbed the bridge of her nose, trying to sort out why this guy had woken her up at six a.m. to chitchat about a case he wasn't remotely involved in prosecuting. "And?"

"And," he cleared this throa,. "we got a tip about it yesterday afternoon. The mugging, I mean."

She must've heard him wrong or she'd lost track of an entire day. He couldn't have gotten a tip about Joule's mugging yesterday afternoon since it hadn't happened until hours later.

She cleared her throat and struggled to find clarity from the fog of sleep. "I think you're mistaken, Sergeant. It happened late last night. Like really late," she said to emphasize this call was disturbing her much needed rest.

"I know it sounds crazy, but I took the call myself. She, the caller, was very specific about the victim and she described your guy perfectly, but when we asked her his name and how she came by the info, she clammed up. We wrote it off until the mugging showed up on the morning tip sheet. I figured you'd at least want to talk to her. I called Vaughn but had to leave a message and the captain suggested I call you directly."

Owen was suddenly very awake. "Has anyone followed up with the woman who called in the tip yet?"

"No. We only just connected the dots and figured you might want to handle it personally."

Owen sighed with relief. "You did the right thing. Send me her contact info." She clicked off the line, and while she waited for the text to come through, she shot off a message to Kira. *Strange new lead. Clear your morning. Meet you at the courthouse in an hour.*

It would be a lot easier to have Kira pick her up again, but she needed to start prioritizing boundaries over convenience. She called down to the valet and asked them to have her car ready, and she checked her phone one more time before heading to the shower. She had one unread message from Sergeant Birken. She clicked on the message, poised for the reveal about their mystery witness, and when the name appeared on the screen, the mystery deepened. *Summer Byrne*—from the jury who'd ruined her perfect streak. What the hell?

CHAPTER SIX

M om, someone's at the door."
Summer looked up from the piece of French toast she'd just flipped on the griddle. Faith was hunched over a textbook at the kitchen table. "Yo, Faith. I can hear the doorbell same as you, but as you can see, I'm a little busy here making sure you have a yummy but decidedly unhealthy breakfast. Any chance you can get the door?"

Faith pointed at her book. "Algebra. It's what's for breakfast."

Nan walked by the kitchen and called out, "I'll get it."

"Thanks," Summer replied. To Faith, she said, "Algebra is not very filling, as I recall. Have some breakfast and then you can get back to it." She held up a plate and then proceeded to fill it with a stack of French toast. "Syrup's over there." She pointed at the counter. "It's the good kind."

Faith dragged her body out of her chair and zombie-walked to the counter. "I guess I can eat. Since you have the good syrup."

Summer laughed and shoved an extra slice onto Faith's plate, determined to make sure she had food in her belly. She'd noticed Faith had become pickier about food since they'd moved. The parade of casseroles had worn out its welcome, and she'd been distracted by the combination of temp work and trying to find a job, but after noticing Faith was looking skinnier than usual, Summer was determined to refocus her efforts on her daughter and make sure she was set up for success here in Dallas. First step, make her favorite breakfast food complete with the fancy maple syrup Faith loved.

"This is amazing," Faith said, stuffing another bite into her mouth. "Best you've ever made. You should maybe open a French toast food truck."

Summer pointed a spatula in her direction. "Now there's an idea. I'll look into that today as soon as you leave for school." They both knew she was kidding, but Faith's grin filled her with warmth. If she could find a job soon, they could get a place of their own. Not that she didn't appreciate Nan taking them in, but moving to Dallas and into Nan's house had been a big adjustment. It had been just the two of them for so long that making the adjustment to include another person had thrown them all off balance. She was ready for things to get back to normal, whatever that was.

As if summoned, Nan reappeared in the kitchen. "Summer, there are some people here to see you." She raised her eyebrows several times in quick succession, widened her eyes, and jerked her thumb, appearing to motion behind her in a way that was only mildly subtle.

"Are you okay?" Summer asked, but as the last word left her mouth, she realized she was the one who wasn't okay. Owen Lassiter, the drop-dead gorgeous prosecutor from the Jex trial, stood framed in the doorway, towering over Nan. "What are you doing here?"

"Mom, that was rude," Faith announced. She stood up and stuck a hand out at Owen, apparently finally finding something more interesting than algebra. "Faith Byrne, nice to meet you."

Summer watched Owen stare at Faith's hand for a second

like it was a coiled snake before she reached out and took it in her own. After they shook, Owen shoved her hand in her pocket as if to signal pleasantries were over, but Faith wasn't one to let go. She turned to Summer. "Firm grip. I like that in a person."

Owen looked disconcerted at the assessment but quickly recovered and grinned at Faith. "Right back at you."

"Are you here to see my mom or Nan?" Faith asked.

"Is your mom Summer Byrne?"

"Yep."

"That's who I'm here to see."

"Who's your friend?"

Owen looked confused for a second, and then turned back to the woman behind her. Also tall. Also gorgeous. Summer sighed. Was she doomed to garner the attention of all the good-looking women in Dallas, but not in a good way?

"This is Kira Vaughn. I'm a prosecutor and she's an investigator who works with me."

Faith nodded as if she understood, and Summer took advantage of the pause in their conversation to step in. "Hey, I'm standing right here, maybe you could talk directly to me instead of my daughter. Again, what are you doing here? Because if you're still hung up on the jury verdict, I assure you I haven't changed my mind and I never will. Showing up at my house uninvited and unannounced is out of bounds, and charming my daughter won't get you anywhere."

Owen winked at Faith. "Your mom thinks I'm charming." She turned back to Summer, her expression now serious. "Actually, I would like to talk to you about a call you made yesterday. It's quite urgent. Is there somewhere we can talk?"

Summer exchanged looks with Nan, who shrugged. She should've known she wouldn't be able to stay under the radar for long, but in her wildest dreams she wouldn't have imagined the phone call she'd made to the police department yesterday would spur Owen Lassiter to show up at her door. She wasn't sure what she would've done differently if she had known, but she definitely would've liked to have had a heads-up this was a possibility.

Owen sniffed the air. "Is something burning?"

"What?" Summer whirled in the direction of the stove in time to see smoke rising from the griddle and the second batch of French toast well on its way to becoming a set of scouring pads. "Damn." She shot a look at Faith. "Sorry."

Faith shrugged. "Guess it's back to algebra for me." She scooped up her textbook. "Mom, we have to leave in thirty minutes, or I'll be late."

Summer silently thanked her for imposing a deadline on the time she'd have to spend with Owen and her sidekick and willed Nan not to interfere by offering to give Faith a ride to school. When Nan settled into a seat at the kitchen table, Summer realized she was way more interested in what Owen and Kira were doing here and she wasn't about to leave. Feeling safety in numbers, Summer motioned for Owen and Kira to have a seat.

"Can I get you something to drink?" she offered, immediately wanting to reel back the words. Why was she offering anything that might cause them to stay longer? *Because you're intrigued by Owen and you have been since you first saw her in the hallway at the courthouse.* She wanted to push the thought aside, deny its truth, but she couldn't. She *was* intrigued by Owen. The vibes she got from Owen told her she was a deep and thoughtful person who was sensitive to other people's feelings and the brash and pushy prosecutor who'd run roughshod over her after the not guilty verdict was a facade.

Kira shook her head, but Owen said, "I'd love coffee if

it's already made. I mean, judging by the breakfast bonanza that's going on here, it looks like it might be made."

Summer narrowed her eyes, looking for a hidden meaning to Owen's words, but Owen's eyes blinked innocently with no sign she meant anything untoward by her remarks. Fine. Summer poured a cup of coffee and asked how she took it.

"Black, please. Good coffee shouldn't be marred with additives. You look like you make good coffee."

Was Owen flirting with her? Why couldn't she say for sure? What use was it to be psychic if, when it came to the most basic things in life, her powers steadfastly refused to kick in?

She thrust the mug at Owen. "Here you go."

Owen sipped from the mug and groaned with pleasure. "Delicious. Thanks."

Summer watched as Owen took another sip, noting the way her lips caressed the outside of the mug before swallowing deeply and ending with a satisfied sigh. She had to do something to distract herself, to end the show of Owen being a pleasure seeking human. "Back to my original question. What are you doing here?"

If Owen thought the question was rude, she didn't let on. "We're investigating a tip received by the Fifth Precinct yesterday. Did you make the call?"

Summer wished the floor would swallow her whole, but no such luck. She'd intended to make her call to the precinct anonymously, but when the duty sergeant had asked her name, the words tumbled out unbidden. She'd written it off as harmless at the time. What were the chances the information would connect to an active case and that they would contact her about it? Apparently, a hundred percent. Her thoughts slammed to a stop. "Wait, you're here."

Owen frowned. "Obviously."

"Which means the tip was good. You wouldn't be here if you thought there was nothing to it. Yes, I made the call." Instinctively, she reached across the table and grasped Owen's forearm. "Did something happen?"

"How about you let us ask the questions?" Kira said, her voice forceful as she looked between them.

"How about you actually ask them instead of barreling into my kitchen acting like you're here because I've done something wrong?" Summer kept her voice calm, but she wasn't about to be pushed around in her own home, even if it was actually her grandmother's house. She stared Kira down and, in the process, started picking up bits of unspoken conversation. *"Don't touch her. Why are you acting so familiar with Owen? Crackpot."* The first two piqued her curiosity, but the last one made her mad. "I'm not a crackpot, no matter what you think."

Kira's eyebrows shot up. Satisfied she'd made her point, Summer faced Owen. "If you want to have a civilized conversation, I'm up for that." She looked at Kira and smiled to soften the sting of their encounter. Kira nodded and she and Owen leaned back in their seats.

Satisfied, Summer asked, "Which one of you wants to tell me what's going on?" She watched Owen shoot a not so subtle look at Kira and then plunge in.

"The duty sergeant at the Fifth Precinct called me this morning to say that he received a call from you yesterday. The content of your call to him was a bit…unusual and we'd like to follow up on it."

While Summer digested the paltry bit of information, she decided to ask some questions of her own. "Kira, are you with the Dallas Police Department?"

Kira looked surprised at the question and she glanced at

Owen, who nodded for her to answer. "I'm an investigator with the district attorney's office."

"Okay." Summer drummed her fingers on the tabletop while she mentally ran through a list of possibilities about why a prosecutor and her investigator would show up on her doorstep over a fairly vague tip about an assault. Only one way to find out. "You're here. Which means there was something to the tip I gave and something relevant either to a case you're working or that you're definitely planning to prosecute, because prosecutors typically don't make house calls for random tips unrelated to any pending investigations. Am I right?"

Owen looked skeptical. *"Someone thinks she's a junior detective."*

"It's not like I think I'm a junior detective or anything," Summer said, taking a bit of satisfaction at the way Owen shifted in her chair when she heard her thoughts spoken out loud. "Seriously, what brought you to my doorstep?"

Owen cleared her throat, and Summer could tell she was stalling for time, probably to decide whether or not she should be honest about why she'd shown up out of the blue or to engage in subterfuge. She prayed for honesty.

"A man matching the description you gave when you called was assaulted last night."

And honesty it was. Summer took a second to revel in her satisfaction before her focus shifted to the fact someone had been injured. "Is he okay?" she asked, and then in response to Owen's startled look. "Are you surprised I would care?"

"No, that's not it," Owen said. "To be perfectly honest, I'm not sure what I expected. What I really want to know is where you got your information that the assault was going to occur."

Okay, here it was. Now it was her turn for honesty, and she braced for their reaction. "I saw it."

"You 'saw' it? You mean you witnessed the assault?" Owen shook her head. "You called it in hours before it happened, so that's impossible."

Summer heard the hard edge of cynicism and considered abandoning any effort to convince Owen how she'd come by her information. But maybe if she told her the truth, Owen and Kira would go away and leave her alone, writing her off as the crazy lady they surely already thought she was. "It's not impossible, actually. I'm a psychic medium." Kira snorted at the words, but Summer pressed on, focusing her attention entirely on Owen. "This isn't the first time I've had a vision about something that turns out to be true."

"Hmm." Owen crossed and uncrossed her arms, a thoughtful expression on her face. "What am I thinking right now?"

"What?"

"If you can read minds, tell me what I'm thinking right now."

Summer's stomach sank and she realized she'd held out some hope Owen would take her at her word, but that hope was dashed now. "It doesn't work that way. I'm not a magic act or a carnival sideshow, ready to perform on command."

"Then how does it work?"

"Things come to me. Dreams, visions, strong intuition. If the details are clear enough, I may be compelled to act."

"So, you got a clear vision of this guy being mugged and you picked up the phone and called the cops?"

"Essentially, yes."

"And we're supposed to believe it's as simple as that?"

"You can believe what you want, but I don't think you'd be here right now if the information I reported wasn't accurate."

"And who's to say you didn't know about the assault because you were involved in it?" Kira asked.

Summer stared her down and then turned back to Owen. "I suppose it's time for you to listen to your own intuition. Does it tell you that I was trying to prevent a crime or that I'm a criminal?" She waited a few beats and when Owen didn't answer, she stood. "Why don't you give it some thought. You can think about it somewhere else, though, because I have things to do and I'd like you both to leave, please."

Kira started to say something, but Owen stood and motioned for her to be quiet. She handed Summer her card. "If you'd like to tell us what really happened, give me a call."

Summer reached for the card, and in the few seconds that she and Owen both held on, the hum of energy was substantial. Owen knew she was telling the truth, but something held her back from admitting it, perhaps even to herself. Summer wanted to talk to her about it, but not in front of Kira who, she was certain, had labeled her a crackpot.

Shortly after they'd left, Summer heard a loud bang of the door. A moment later, Nan poked her head in the kitchen, her eyebrows raised in a question. "Come on in. They're gone. I'm making a fresh batch of French toast because I deserve it after being interrogated. You want some?"

"Is 'no' ever a proper response to that question?" Nan asked with a grin. "Tell me everything."

"There's not much to tell. They were stingy with intel, but my dream was spot-on."

"That tall one is pretty dreamy, if you ask me. What was her name? Owen? Unusual, but interesting. I bet it's a family name. It suits her. And speaking of suits, she knows how to dress, that one does." *"You should invite her back for dinner."*

Summer felt the warmth of a blush creep up her neck and she waved a spatula at Nan. "Stop it. Stop it right now. That was not a social call. Owen is working on some case that involves the guy who was mugged. Plus, she was the prosecutor when I had jury duty last week. The one who thought I wrecked the jury and robbed her of the right verdict."

"Too many coincidences there. She's in your life for a reason."

Summer focused on the routine of dipping the bread in the batter and placing it on the hot griddle to keep from dwelling on the fact she was having the very same thoughts. Every encounter with Owen felt both new and familiar, and the intrigue was exciting and frightening at the same time. "I know you think you're in the business of dispensing wisdom by virtue of your status as the older woman in the house, but sometimes a coincidence is simply that and has no deep-seated meaning."

"You know better than that, but I suppose you have to come to the correct conclusion on your own in order to embrace it as real."

"Whatever." Summer knew she was right. The way all of her synapses had lit up when she came into contact with Owen told her there was more to their connection than simple happenstance. What she didn't know was whether their connection was related only to this case or to something more personal. The real question was, did she want to find out?

❖

"Do you think it was a good idea to let her off the hook so easily?" Kira asked as they pulled away from Summer's house.

"What did you want me to do, hold a gun to her head?" Owen stared back at the house, wishing she'd visited on her own, without Kira, and wondering if she should go back and give talking to Summer another go. She didn't believe for a moment that Summer had psychic abilities, but her gut told her Summer wasn't being dishonest, and Owen wasn't sure how to reconcile the two opposing views. Plus, she'd felt something during their conversation—the kind of thing she often felt in the courtroom when she knew exactly what to ask a witness or when to call some testimony into question based on pure instinct. Her instinct was telling her now that Summer knew more about her case than she was letting on. The major question was why Summer had chosen to keep her knowledge to herself.

Owen wrested her gaze from the house. Her imagination was running wild, another distraction to keep her from focusing on Fuentes as the sole suspect in Mrs. Adams's murder. The police had arrested him, the grand jury had indicted him, and his case was set for trial in less than two weeks. She hadn't prepped the case from the beginning, but it was hers now and her only job was to give the citizens of Dallas the justice they deserved for the death of Commissioner Adams's wife. "This was a waste of time," she muttered.

"What's that?"

Owen shook her head. "Nothing. Will you drop me at the office? Rivera wants a full report, and I want you to check on Joule."

Kira held up her phone. "Franco texted about ten minutes ago. All is well."

"I'd appreciate it if you would check. Personally." Owen injected extra force into her words to convey the subject was closed.

Kira's jaw hardened and her hands tightened on the steering wheel. "Fine. I get it."

Owen hoped she meant it. She should confront Kira more directly about the blurred boundaries between them, but despite her reputation as a badass at the courthouse, she didn't want to hurt Kira's feelings. Instead she resolved to ensure their interactions remained professional—no more happy hour flings and no more having Kira pick her up at home out of convenience.

The courthouse was still buzzing with the business of the morning docket, but Owen flashed her badge and cut in front of the long line of people waiting to get in the front door. She used to feel bad about jumping the line, but it had only taken a few weeks of waiting behind people who didn't understand the concept of how to empty their pockets and what might set off a metal detector to convince her to take advantage of the convenience her badge afforded her. She rode the escalator to the fourth floor and then slipped into the stairwell to climb the remaining three flights to her boss's office.

The suite of offices afforded to the elected DA and her first assistant took up a large portion of the eleventh floor. Owen knew they needed extra space for meetings with staff and important public officials, but she wondered how hard it was to stay in touch with what was going on in the rest of the office when you were shelved in quiet seclusion, away from the seedy side of criminal prosecution. She had absolutely no interest in working her way into this cocoon. Teaching younger prosecutors was a duty she'd learned to embrace, and she actually enjoyed it, but that was as far removed from litigation as she ever wanted to be.

DA Mia Rivera's secretary, Henry, was sitting outside her door when Owen approached. "I've been summoned," she said with a smile she didn't feel. "Is she in?"

"She is, but you're early."

"I was told to show up immediately, so you could argue I'm right on time."

Henry nodded. "Gunning for a promotion." He wagged a finger at Owen. "I know the look. Crisp suit, first one at the office, last one to leave. She'll be impressed for sure."

Owen didn't bother denying the assumption. She was already the youngest attorney to be promoted to a chief position and she appreciated Mia's confidence in her work, but she hadn't been prepared for how much she would miss time spent in the courtroom, lost to all the administrative work that went with supervising a bunch of misdemeanor prosecutors.

"She's ready for you now."

Owen stood and smoothed the lines in her suit. Mia Rivera had been her mentor when she'd started this job and she was ever conscious about impressing her, especially now that she was in this new position. When she walked in, Mia was on the phone and held up a finger to signal she'd be just a minute. While she waited, Owen took a moment to glance around the room that had been occupied by so many men before Mia had won the last election, becoming the first female DA in Dallas. Framed pictures illustrated the diverse support Mia had received from every corner of Dallas, bringing together a coalition of voters that were more interested in finding a new approach to law and order than doing things the same old way, and Owen was proud to be a part of the changes Mia was making as part of her mandate. They were no longer prosecuting everything that came through the door, instead focusing on alternative justice programs that included special programs for first time offenders, drug counseling, and other rehabilitative programs. The result was the prosecutors weren't mired down with petty crimes, but instead able to focus on taking dangerous criminals off the streets.

"Thanks for all the info," Mia said into the phone. "Much appreciated." She hung up and turned her attention to Owen.

"Sit. Please. Do you want some coffee? I hear you were out late and up early."

Owen slid into the chair across from Mia's desk. "I'm good, thanks. Kira just sent me a text that Joule is in good condition, but I have a feeling you already knew that."

Mia smiled. "How well you know me. I got here early too and have been doing some investigating of my own. What was your impression of Summer Byrne?"

Owen fixed her face into a neutral expression. She should've anticipated Mia would already know about Summer's tip—it was very much like her to be hands-on when it came to big cases. She wanted to blurt out that Summer had mucked up her jury trial last week and dashed her perfect record, but she knew Mia valued moving on as opposed to dwelling on the past, so she needed to tread carefully here. "Kira and I met with her this morning. Frankly, I'm not sure what to think. Her information was certainly credible, but her explanation of how she came by it, is more incredible than anything else."

"She's a psychic medium."

"That's her claim anyway."

"No, she really is." Mia turned her computer screen so Owen could see. "Her name rang a bell and I did some checking around. She has quite the reputation on the West Coast. I was on the phone with the elected DA in Santa Cruz, Bruce Janney. I heard him speak at a law enforcement conference last year about unorthodox crime solving techniques and he mentioned Summer. He said she was invaluable in helping them solve cases for several years and the law enforcement agencies out there would back him up on that. She even got a mention on an episode of *Dateline*."

"Wow, that's interesting." Owen hoped her voice conveyed more enthusiasm than she felt. She had no interest in stories about special powers when she had real facts to find and factor in the preparation of her case.

"I want to bring her in. Set up a meeting and see if she'd be willing to work with you on the Adams case. Based on what I've learned, she could be invaluable all the way from jury selection to assessing the witnesses during trial. We have some extra funds from the seizure of all those eight-liner machines last month. We can't offer her a ton, but we can do a decent stipend."

"What?" Owen wasn't entirely sure she'd heard Mia correctly. "You want to hire her to work on the Adams case? But that case is already solved, remember?"

"Yes, I want her to work with you on the Adams case. And it may be solved, but you still have to convince a jury. In fact, that's the perfect cover. You can tell people she's on board as a jury consultant. Assuming she'll agree to work with us. I'm sure you can be persuasive."

Owen bit her bottom lip while she contemplated responses other than "hell no," which was the only one that readily came to mind. Mia was clearly excited about her discovery, but Owen's skepticism was firmly entrenched. Deciding that attacking the whole psychic medium angle might not be the best way to get her doubt across, she tried another tack. "She was the foreperson in the case I tried with Ben Green last week. The one where the jury went rogue."

"Rogue?" Mia raised her eyebrows. "Look, Owen, I know you've never lost before, but juries are famous for making decisions based on the most random factors. Judge DeWhitt said you made your best case, but it doesn't always pan out."

"She was clearly biased for the defense."

"Judge Dewitt?"

Owen tempered her tone. "No, Summer Byrne. And don't you think it's odd that not a week after being on jury duty, she just happens to have critical information about an assault on the star witness in a headliner case? You said she was on TV. Maybe she's gunning for media attention."

Even as she spoke the words, Owen knew they didn't jibe with the woman she'd met that morning, making French toast while helping her kid do algebra. Summer had seemed extremely matter-of-fact, completely at odds with the picture Owen had in her head of a dramatic fortune teller presiding over a seance. Still, she didn't buy that Summer channeled information from the great beyond or had visions that foretold the future. That kind of fortune-teller shit had no place in the fact-finding world she occupied.

"If she were looking for attention, don't you think she would've called the press and not the police? Besides, I said she was mentioned on an episode of *Dateline*. She wasn't on the show. Bruce told me that despite the fact she worked on some high-profile cases, she never appeared on TV— something about keeping her life as private as possible. She has a young daughter. Does that sound like a publicity hound to you?"

Mia had a point, but Owen wasn't ready to concede defeat. "I met her this morning. Kira and I went by her house to see what she could tell us. Not much other than what she described when she called it in, but she didn't strike me as particularly helpful."

"She might respond more amicably if you didn't show up on her doorstep unannounced. And we're willing to pay her for her assistance. Your job is to convince her to come on board."

"I'm thinking an overture from you would have a better chance of being well-received. I don't think she likes me very much."

"Is that your extrasensory powers at work?"

"Evidence based on empirical data."

"I've seen you charm dozens of guilty verdicts out of juries." Mia stood to signal the meeting was over and made a shooing motion. "You're going to have to work closely with her for the duration of the trial, so it should be you. She's got to learn you aren't a total disbeliever. Go forth and be the persuasive advocate that you are."

Owen wanted to protest, wanted to tell Mia she wouldn't do it, that she'd never believe in the mumbo jumbo Summer was selling, but she'd known Mia long enough to recognize when her mind was made up. Plus, she knew that Mia was placing a lot of confidence in her by asking her to step in and handle the Adams case, but as much as Mia liked her, she wouldn't hesitate to rip it away if she felt it wasn't getting prosecuted the way she wanted. Owen sighed. She didn't really have a choice, and a part of her was glad about it. Now she just had to figure out how to get Summer to like her enough to agree to help, and the prospect was both challenging and exciting.

CHAPTER SEVEN

"What were the cops doing here this morning? Are you going to work with them again?"

Summer looked up from the pot roast she'd just pulled out of the oven and met Faith's intense gaze. They'd never talked in-depth about the work she'd done for law enforcement in Santa Cruz, but they had talked about her gift, and Faith was a smart girl, which meant she'd likely figured out the gist. "I saw something the other day and I called in a tip. They were following up to make sure they had all the information they needed. And they weren't cops. Owen's a prosecutor and Kira is the investigator assigned to work with her."

"Oh yeah, I remember. Owen's the tall, dreamy one. Sharp dresser."

It was like Faith was reading her mind. Surprise. "I suppose. I was too busy burning the rest of the French toast to notice."

"She was nice. Talked to me like a person, not a kid."

"Of course she did. Kids are people too."

"You know that, and I know that, but other people not so much."

"What is it that we know?" Nan asked as she walked into the room.

"Nothing," Summer said at the same moment Faith blurted out, "We're talking about the dreamy lawyer who came to see Mom this morning."

"The tall one? Definitely dreamy. Sharp dresser too."

Faith stuck her tongue out at Summer. "See!"

Summer shook her head. "You two are hilarious." She poured off some liquid from the roast into a frying pan and stirred in some flour. "Dinner will be ready in ten minutes. Faith, go ahead and set the table, please."

Summer watched her pretend-huff off toward the cabinets and pulled down three plates. Back in Santa Cruz, more often than not, they would load their dinner onto TV trays and eat in the living room, but Nan insisted they take their meals together at the table, and Summer could tell Faith liked the tradition no matter how much she might protest.

She'd learned to like it too. No TV, no phones, no connecting to the outside world in any way for at least one hour while they shared a meal and real conversation—the kind that happened when they were looking at each other instead of a screen. The routine had helped to calm her thoughts at the end of a long day of temp work or looking for a job, and she'd felt more peaceful since the move because of it. Until Leo Joule had popped into her head with his near-death assault.

She'd combed the news and finally found a picture of Joule. He was an important witness in the murder case of Commissioner Adams's wife, and he was definitely the man she'd seen at the courthouse after she'd talked to Owen. Summer hadn't stopped there. She'd spent the afternoon scouring the internet for information about the murder of Carrie Adams. Owen had recently been assigned to head the prosecution team on the case, and the trial was set to start in two weeks. Everyone predicted the defendant would go to prison for the rest of his life. Summer was a little surprised they weren't seeking the death penalty, but secretly she was glad. No matter what someone was accused of, the system could be fallible, and when a life was at stake, there should be no margin of error. She was well acquainted with what could happen when mistakes were made and lives hung in the balance. Thank goodness she didn't have to deal with that kind of pressure anymore. She'd gladly trade temp work for life-and-death decisions, any day of the week.

"Mom, you're stirring the gravy to death. People are starving here."

She looked up to see Faith and Nan sitting at the perfectly set table, loaded with all the food she'd prepared, sans gravy. "Sorry. Be right there."

"Use the fancy gravy boat," Nan called out. "This is a pretty fancy meal for a weeknight. It's in the cabinet over the sink."

Summer dutifully complied and joined them at the table.

"This *is* pretty special," Faith said. "What's the occasion, Mom?"

Before she could answer, the doorbell rang. Faith wagged a finger. "No interruptions during dinner. I didn't make the rules."

Summer opened her mouth to answer, but before she could speak, the bell rang again. "I'll get it. P.S. It's not my fault your great-grandmother lives in the kind of neighborhood where people drop by." She grinned. "Heathens."

When she reached the door, she peeked through the viewer and her breath caught when she spotted Owen Lassiter pacing on the porch. Before she could give it another thought, she swung open the door. "Did you not get all your digs in this morning or do you make a hobby out of showing up on people's doorsteps unannounced?"

Owen grimaced and she ducked her head in a move

that appeared to convey humility, surprising considering her courtroom swagger. She held up her phone. "I tried calling, but no one answered and your voice mail is full. May I come in?"

Summer hesitated a moment. Owen did look somewhat contrite in addition to dashing, and the connection she'd felt earlier was still strong. She wondered what would happen if she touched Owen's arm. Would her mind light up with images or would she simply feel the warmth that Owen was really, really good at hiding? "Actually, if I invited you in, I'd be breaking the rules, and—"

"Oh, so you *do* believe in rules," Owen said with a grin. "Your rogue nature must be confined to jury duty."

"Hey, that's not fair." Summer stared at Owen's smile, marveling at the way it went all the way to her eyes, but before she could say more, Faith's voice bellowed from within the house.

"Mom, who is it? Dinner's getting cold."

She squeezed her forehead. "I'm trying to remember if I blurted out my every thought when I was twelve."

Owen backed away. "I interrupted your dinner. Trust me, I'm not usually this rude. You have my number. I'd really appreciate it if you would give me a call. I have something very important to ask you."

"Wait." Summer paused for a moment, unsure what else to say, but sure she didn't want Owen to dash off. She was getting a completely different vibe off this version of her. More…human? She was saved from having to figure out words when Faith appeared at her side.

Faith waved a hand and grinned. "Hi, Owen."

Owen grinned again. "Hi, Faith." She waved a hand. "Sorry I interrupted your dinner."

Faith lit up at the attention. "Mom made pot roast."

"I can smell it from here." Owen sniffed the air. "It smells amazing."

Faith nodded eagerly. "It looks delicious and there's a ton. Have you eaten?"

She switched her attention to Summer, who hid her discomfort behind a smile, while blinking at Faith in an attempt to signal her to shut up. If reading minds was really genetic, then her daughter had either been switched at birth or seriously needed to hone her skills.

"Uh, well…"

Summer looked at Owen, who was visibly uncomfortable at being put on the spot, and in that moment, she glimpsed the vulnerability she'd felt when she'd touched Owen's arm at the courthouse. Before she could change her mind, she blurted out, "You should join us. There's plenty of food, and I'm a decent cook."

"Nan says it's super fancy for a school night," Faith added.

"It's not all that fancy," Summer said.

Owen raised her hands. "Who needs fancy?"

Summer gestured at Owen's outfit. "Said the fancy dresser."

Owen grinned. "You like the way I dress."

The swagger was back, and Summer recognized it for the cover it was. But what was Owen trying to hide? She shook her head. It wasn't her job to analyze Owen. She was here on business. Okay, so they were about to share a meal, but it was a business dinner, the kind that happened all the time where bread was broken and deals were struck and everyone walked away with something they wanted. So, why did she feel like only one of them was going to walk away happy?

❖

Owen followed Summer into the house, trying her best to take in the surroundings, but Faith was at her side delivering a steady stream of questions.

"Mom says you're a prosecutor. That means you go to trial a lot, right? What's the hardest case you've ever worked on? Do you ever get scared that the people you send to jail are going to come get you when they get out?"

"Faith, cool it," Summer said. "Owen isn't here for you to interview."

"What if she doesn't mind?" Faith asked.

"I don't mind," Owen said at the same time. "Seriously."

"At least let her eat first." Summer stopped when they arrived at the kitchen where Nan was standing near the entry. "Go ahead and get back in your seat, Nan. I'm sure you heard every word."

Nan huffed as she sat down. "Not every word, but I did hear enough to tell me we needed another place setting." She pointed at the extra spot at the table. "Hi, Owen, it's nice to see you again."

"Hi, Mrs....?"

Nan stuck out her hand. "Harvey, Helen Harvey."

"Hi, Mrs. Harvey. It's nice to see you too."

"Don't call me Mrs. It makes me irritable. Call me Nan." Nan leaned over to Summer. "She's very polite."

"And I bet she has decent hearing too," Summer said, flashing a smile at Owen. "How about we try to act like a normal family while we eat?"

"As if." Nan handed the platter of pot roast to Owen and pointed at a large section. "Take that. You look like someone who's been eating whatever they could fish out of a vending machine. A real meal would do you good. Have some extra carrots too. Summer is a wonderful cook."

"I can tell," Owen said as she took the piece of pot roast

and more carrots than she would probably eat in an effort to appease Nan, who was staring her down like a drill sergeant. "I must admit, I've been working a lot lately and haven't had a home-cooked meal in a while."

"Is there someone at home who cooks for you?"

"Nan!" Summer shook her head. "In case you didn't hear when you had your ear pressed against the wall, Owen is here on business. Try to have a few boundaries, please."

"I don't mind the questions," Owen said. "I spend most of my time asking them, so it's fun to get to answer once in a while." She turned back to Nan. "Occasionally, I use a service to have prepared meals cooked to order and sent over so I can store them in my freezer. Does that count?"

"Hmm," Nan said, tapping the table with her fingers like she was trying to think of another question to ask.

"It doesn't count," Summer said. "Not for what she's thinking. Would you like something to drink? Sorry, I'm usually a much better hostess. We've got iced tea, soda, water. I might be able to rustle up some wine from Nan's not-so-secret stash."

"Tea would be great. And it wasn't like I gave you any warning for my visit," Owen said, stabbing a forkful of the pot roast. The tender meat practically melted in her mouth. "And for the record, I didn't expect you to roll out the red carpet when I arrived, but I'm glad you did because this is the best meal I've had in a long time."

Summer blushed slightly at the compliment. "Thanks. I'm between jobs and I've been watching a lot of cooking shows."

They spent the next half hour digging into dinner and discussing innocuous subjects like the weather and the upcoming state fair. Owen devoured her food and barely managed to resist Nan's efforts to fill her plate a second time. She pushed her plate away. "That was amazing, but I'm full."

She mentally cast about for a way to broach the subject of her visit, but Faith saved her from the dilemma.

"What did you want to ask my mom?"

Owen looked at Summer who gave her a slight nod. "I, we, need your mom's help on a case. She already helped me some this morning, but I could use her expertise again. I understand she used to work with law enforcement agencies where you used to live."

"Yes, she did," Faith said. "She was good at it. She helped them solve all but one case."

Owen noted the odd coincidence that Summer had had exactly as many losses as her. Was it possible Mia had been on to something, forcing her to find a way to involve Summer in this case? "Only one case unsolved is a pretty amazing accomplishment," Owen said, conscious of the irony since she saw her one loss as a huge blemish on her own record. She glanced at Summer, whose expression was now completely devoid of affect. "Did I say something wrong?"

Faith nodded. "She doesn't like to talk about it."

"Faith, do me a favor and go out to the garage and get the ice cream out of the freezer."

Faith let out a big sigh and stood. "You could just say, 'Hey, I need a minute to talk to Owen in private.'"

"True, but then you wouldn't be able to tell me how smart you are for figuring out what I really meant."

"Fine, but I don't think it's fair that Nan gets to stay."

"Nan's going to help you." Summer made a shooing motion and Faith trudged out of the room with Nan close behind. Once they were out of sight, Summer turned to Owen. "Why are you really here?"

Surprised at the question, Owen set down her fork and crossed her hands. "I told you. We need your help on a case."

"I find that hard to believe since you don't believe in my

abilities. Not to mention the fact you think that I—how did you put it? I have no respect for the rule of law."

Owen should've known better than to argue with Summer about the Jex case. It was a rookie mistake, but she'd had no idea at the time she'd be charged with asking Summer for a favor soon after. She had some sucking up to do. "Clearly, I was wrong. I've read about your work with the Santa Cruz DA and the police and sheriff's office out there. They all have only good things to say about you and the work you did with them."

Summer's eyes narrowed a bit like she was skeptical. "What exactly do you want?"

Owen summoned all the sincerity she could muster, praying Summer wouldn't be able to read the disbelief below the surface. "I assume you've heard about the murder of Commissioner Adams's wife?" At Summer's nod, she continued. "It's set for trial in two weeks. We'd like to bring you on board to consult with us. Meet with witnesses for pretrial prep, sit through jury selection and the trial and give us your opinions on how we're doing and your impressions of the defense and the evidence represented. We will pay you for your time."

"And if you don't agree with what I have to say?"

"Well, as the lead prosecutor on the case, I'll have the final say, but I promise I'll consider any advice you have to offer." Owen smiled to punctuate her remarks and hopefully appear to be the kind of lawyer open to other people's opinions, but the truth was if there was a showdown, she wasn't about to take the advice of a woo-woo medium over her own well-honed litigation skills no matter what Mia wanted.

"Right." Summer looked skeptical.

"You don't believe me."

"Now look who's a mind reader? No, I do not, but it

doesn't matter what I believe. I don't do that kind of work anymore."

"Why not?" Owen was genuinely curious.

"I just don't. That was another life, another place, another time. I'm very busy now. Too busy to work with you even if I wanted to, which I do not. I'm sorry you wasted your time coming by."

Owen wanted to argue the point, use her powers of persuasion to convince Summer to divulge the reason behind her reluctance, but Summer's frown and obvious agitation held her back. Instead she pointed at her empty plate and attempted some levity. "No need to apologize. This may be the most delicious meal I've ever had."

The easy smile returned to Summer's face. "Well, I'm not sure that's saying much since Nan is convinced you never eat. You should wear a few extra layers next time you see her to get her to lay off the 'You're so skinny, you need to eat more' routine." Summer's hand flew to her mouth. "Not to imply you're going to see her again. Wait, that sounded bad. Of course, you can see her anytime you want. I only meant it's not likely, you know, since…"

As if on cue, Nan and Faith appeared in the doorway. Faith was holding a baking pan and Nan was holding a bucket of Blue Bell vanilla ice cream. "Dessert, anyone?" Nan asked, brandishing a scoop. "Summer made blackberry cobbler."

Owen considered her options. She wasn't going to get what she'd come for, and as much as she'd enjoyed the meal and the company, sticking around for more felt disingenuous in a way she couldn't quite articulate. She pushed her chair back and set her napkin on the table. "I should probably go."

"Please don't go," Faith said. "I helped make the cobbler. Well, I helped pick the blackberries, which I think counts as helping. If you leave, we won't have an independent third-party opinion about whether it's good or not."

"Not to mention, you don't look like you allow yourself to eat dessert ever," Nan said, "and that's a damn shame."

Owen laughed and glanced at Summer, who was shaking her head in surrender. "You really should stay for dessert," Summer said. "It's a new recipe, so I can't vouch for how good it is, but an unbiased opinion would be welcome."

Owen considered the offer carefully. If she stayed, she could use the time to try to convince Summer to change her mind. She'd be doing her job, doing exactly what Mia wanted her to do, but Summer hadn't been waffling when she said she wasn't interested. No, she had been quite firm on the subject. If Owen had really wanted her help on the case, a little resistance wouldn't stop her, but she had absolutely no desire to add another person to the team, especially one who had nothing to contribute except unfiltered feelings, source unknown. "It's tempting, but I really do need to go." She pushed in her chair and pointed at her plate. "Should I put this in the sink?"

"Guests don't clean," Faith said. "That's what Mom says anyway."

"It's true," Summer said. "It's a rule. Faith, why don't you say good-bye to Owen and then I'll walk her to the door?"

Owen was surprised as everyone else appeared to be that Summer would see her out. She shook Faith's hand, thanked Nan for her hospitality, and followed Summer to the door. "Thank you. Dinner was delicious."

"You're welcome," Summer said. "And I truly am sorry I can't help you out."

"My boss will be very disappointed," Owen said. *And I'm sorry I won't have an excuse to see you again.* "She was looking forward to meeting you."

Summer looked down. "That's not my life anymore."

Owen wanted to ask why, not as a way to find leverage to get Summer to work on the Adams case, but because she genuinely wanted to know more about the source of the pain in Summer's eyes when she mentioned her past. But as much as she'd enjoyed an evening spent pretending to be part of Summer's happy little family, coming here had been a job, and now she needed to report back to her boss that her mission had been unsuccessful. She might have shown up hoping Summer would turn her down, but she was leaving with an unusual feeling of regret, and as she looked one more time into Summer's eyes, she wondered if Summer knew exactly what she was thinking.

CHAPTER EIGHT

Summer could hear her phone ringing, but other than being able to tell from the proximity of the sound it was somewhere in the den, she couldn't find it. She really should keep the damn thing tethered to her wrist, especially since she was expecting a call from the headhunter who'd been trying to land her a paralegal position in one of the big downtown law firms. The kind of position that specialized in something boring, like tax or oil or securities—anything but criminal law.

She finally located the phone in between the couch cushions and jabbed the answer button before the caller gave up on reaching her. "Hello, this is Summer."

"Hi, Summer. It's Bruce."

Summer held the phone away from her ear and stared at the screen. If she hadn't been such a mess, leaving her phone stuck in the couch, she might've spent a second checking the screen before she answered and noticed the number was from out of state. It had been three months since she'd heard his voice and she still wasn't ready.

"Are you still there?"

She let out a deep breath. "Yes, I'm here."

"Are you doing okay?"

She sank onto the couch and considered the question. She

was healthy, she had a roof over her head and food on the table and family that loved her, or at least a tiny portion of a family. But since the move from California, she'd been out of sorts. Wait, that wasn't right. Her discomfort had started before the move, and Bruce's voice on the other line brought it all roaring back. "I'm making do." It was the most honest answer she could offer.

"Thanks for answering," he said, a tinge of relief in his voice. "I didn't like how we left things and I've wanted to talk to you, but I've been trying to give you your space."

"What changed?" Before he could answer, an image of the Dallas County courthouse popped into her head. She didn't know the connection between Bruce Diaz, her former boss, and the case Owen had come to see her about, but she knew there was one. "Wait, I know why you're calling."

He laughed. "Of course you do. The question is will you do me this favor?"

"You want me to work with the prosecutor here the same way I worked for you?"

"Yes."

She'd hoped she was wrong, but now that she knew she wasn't, all she could think about was what was in it for him?

"You're probably wondering why I'm asking," he said.

"Oh, look who's reading minds now."

"Just an educated guess. The DA out there, Mia Rivera, called and offered to loan me the guy who set up their in-house forensic lab and help me write a grant proposal similar to the one they used to get federal funding. Mia's a rising star, and with her assistance, we might finally get a state-of-the-art system that will keep us from having to wait on the backlogged state lab for forensic testing."

"And she'll help you if I help her?"

"I didn't make her any promises. She asked me to talk

to you—that's it. But that's not the only reason I called. She explained that you reached out to the local police about what you...saw. The fact you were willing to pick up the phone and make the call is a sign you're not done using your talents. What happened here was completely out of your control. Your gift may be fallible, but without it, there's no telling how many criminals would still be walking the streets."

"I wish I believed you."

"You should. This is your calling. I got a call for a reference for you last week from some business lawyer looking for a paralegal. You may think getting a job like that will be satisfying, but I can guarantee you will spend your days wondering if the dreams you have are driving you to a higher purpose."

Summer heard the conviction in his voice and was certain it came from personal experience, but she had personal experience of her own, which was precisely why she was reluctant to get involved in this kind of work again. She closed her eyes and remembered the last case she worked in Santa Cruz. The dream was vivid still. The girl, Violet Laramore, had been two years younger than Faith, but unlike Faith, she was frail and delicate, having been sick with cancer for most of her life. Her kidnapping had caused an uproar in the community with everyone questioning what kind of monster would harm such a helpless creature. Parents locked their kids indoors and held them close.

Like everyone else, Summer was surrounded by the daily drumbeat of reporting speculating on possible scenarios for the missing girl, which surely factored into her dreams. Dreams about Violet. Locked in a closet. In a house. In the woods. What woods, what house? She'd been certain she knew, but she'd only been close, and close wasn't good enough when moments mattered in the race between life and death. When they finally found Violet, paramedics had worked hard to revive her, but it was too late, and with her death, Summer's peaceful, happy life had imploded.

She reached for her neck, remembering the collar Violet's kidnapper had used to restrain the young girl, and she choked out a response. "I don't know, Bruce. We're getting a new start here, keeping a low profile."

"Yet you still made the call to the police," he said. "Summer, you and I both know you can't turn it off. You know this will keep happening, right? You'll see things, you'll get messages you won't be able to ignore. I know you."

He did know her, as well as anyone could. She'd spent so much of her life hiding her gift, hiding what she was able to see in an effort to be normal, but the first time she'd reached out to him, he had believed her. She hadn't expected it, had been prepared for rejection, but the impetus was so strong, she couldn't deny its pull. They'd worked together for several years, and then for the first time in her life, she felt normal, like the thoughts in her head and the feelings that drove her to see beyond what was in this realm were not distractions, but instead they were her destiny. She'd had purpose then, but since she'd left Santa Cruz, she'd had none. Sure, she felt worth as Faith's mother, but she was floundering to find her place and she knew that affected Faith as well.

"It's not like you're using your talents to entertain people. You have the opportunity to help make the world a safer place. It's a calling."

Summer knew he was speaking from the heart, but she suspected there was more to his request than he'd let on. "Not to mention it would help you out if I did this favor for you."

"True, but I'm thinking it would help us both out. I

wouldn't have called if I thought otherwise. Will you at least think about it? Talk to Mia and hear what she has to say? I promise you, she's a true believer."

She owed him as much. After news broke in Santa Cruz that Bruce and the police had used a "secret weapon" to help them find Violet Laramore, the press found out Bruce had been using her for years to help with cases on his docket. Her name, her entire life, had become fodder for the media, and after her failure to save Violet, headlines like *DA Relies on Psychic Instead of Good Sense* and *Medium Justice Gets Minimal Results* emblazoned across the local paper. Experts on the evening news pontificated about how disembodied voices and visions that only one woman could see didn't constitute real evidence. While she'd been dogged by reporters who wanted to know every last detail of her personal life, Bruce had taken the brunt of the criticism for hiring and relying on her in the first place while he stood steadfast in support of her staying on in her capacity as a consultant. No one else in her life, besides Nan, had ever been so loyal and protective. "I'll think about it."

"Thank you." A few seconds passed. "We miss you here. If you ever decide to come back, there's a place for you."

It wasn't going to happen. She missed so much about that life. The quaint town of Santa Cruz, the ocean, the pier. Dallas was a huge, landlocked city, with only man-made lakes to satisfy her longing for water. But no one knew her here. No one had any preconceived expectations of her, of her abilities, of her success. She was simply Summer Byrne without any modifier like "medium" or "psychic" to color people's expectations, and she was determined to keep it that way.

After she hung up from talking to Bruce, she went out to the backyard and wandered through Nan's flower garden. Nan liked to pretend that her grandfather, Charlie, was the only one who'd ever done any work around the house, from cooking to cleaning to handyman repairs, but her green thumb brought the backyard to life in a magical way. The yard was full of features from an arbor wound with wisteria to a charming butterfly garden with a wrought iron bench surrounded by vintage rosebushes. Summer loved the random chaos of this oasis. It was the polar opposite of the neatly trimmed gardens of her parents' house in Houston, tended to by a team of gardeners who cared more about the money they made than creating beauty in nature. Not for the first time she wondered how someone like Nan had raised a daughter who was her opposite in every way.

She heard the door open and looked up from the roses to see Nan walking toward her. She pointed at the seat beside her. "Mind if I join you?" She'd barely sat down when she started talking about the garden. "It's time for more mums, don't you think? And maybe we should set some pumpkins out over there." Nan pointed at a spot in the corner of the yard. "Add a few hay bales and it's a regular fall festival. Speaking of festivals, do you think Faith would like to go to the arboretum for the fall displays? It's not really a teenager kind of thing, but she seems like she enjoys being in the garden."

"She'd love it," Summer said with confidence, thankful her own daughter liked many of the same things she did. "But you've treated us to enough while we're here. Hopefully, I'll get a call from the headhunter soon and be gainfully employed. Then I can treat you to some things you enjoy."

Nan waved her off. "Don't be silly. I'm an old widow, and I'm lucky enough to have the pleasure of a grandkid and great-grandkid hanging out with me. Now, that is something I enjoy. Not everyone is lucky enough to have family they actually like, let alone can live with. And I have plenty of money. If I want to spend it on treating my favorite relatives to some fun, that's exactly what I'll do. Understood?"

"Understood." Summer knew it was senseless to argue the point.

"And while we're on the subject of doing what we want, I want to talk to you about this job search. Are you really planning to work for one of those blood-sucking, white shoe law firms downtown?"

"I don't think they suck actual blood or wear white shoes, but if you're asking if I'm up for a job with a large, financially solvent firm that pays good salaries and provides top-tier benefits, the answer is yes. Is there a problem with that?"

"Not if you fancy selling your soul to the highest bidder."

Her sentiment echoed Bruce's words, and Summer blurted out, "My old boss called today."

"He wants you to come back."

Nan's words were declarative, but Summer heard an edge of apprehension in her voice. "He said I was welcome to, but that's not going to happen."

"So, he wanted something else?"

"Yes. Owen's boss contacted him, asked him to help persuade me to help on this case they have going to trial. Commissioner Adams's wife was murdered."

"Yes, it was all over the news when it happened. What are you going to do?"

"Hope the headhunter calls with an offer."

"You already have a calling." Nan gestured around the yard. "I know you would probably rather have your own place, but you and Faith are welcome to stay here for as long as you like. Permanently, even. To be honest, given how your mother doesn't like me, I never thought we'd have the opportunity to have a relationship of any kind, and now that you're here, I can't imagine this house without you and Faith in it." She shook her head. "But it's not about me. It's about what's best for you two. If you think taking a 'regular' job is going to make you happy—do it. But if you can find the strength to reconnect with who you are, the gift you have—however imperfect it might be—then embracing it might give you more freedom than punching a clock for a big paycheck."

Summer closed her eyes and let the emotion behind Nan's words wrap her in their warmth. Nan's acceptance, her understanding, meant more than the acceptance she'd experienced from Bruce and the others she'd worked with in Santa Cruz because there was no quid pro quo. Nan understood the pros and cons of the gift and had no expectations it would benefit her in any way. No, Nan only wanted what was best for her and Faith, and Summer knew without a doubt her feelings were genuine, which was precisely why her own mother had kept them apart. She'd missed years of being able to be in the presence of someone who got her, who encouraged her to develop her skills instead of hide them as a freakish anomaly. What had happened in Santa Cruz had scarred her for sure, but did it have to define who she would be?

"I want to stay," she said. "This house feels like home. And I want Faith to have a relationship with you. We're family. You're all the family I have."

"Then stay. And you can do whatever you want to earn a living. I didn't mean to be a control freak about that."

Summer smiled at hearing Nan say the words "control freak." "Well, maybe I will give the DA's office a call and hear them out. They did say they were willing to pay."

"Don't forget the bonus of getting to work with Owen."

Nan wagged her finger at her. "You two have a connection. She may act like she doesn't believe in your gift, but she's a deep one. She'll come around."

I haven't forgotten. Not sure I'd agree otherwise.

Chapter Nine

Owen stared at the white board like she had every day for the past week, but the result was the same. The evidence was straightforward and simple, but she still had doubts, and if she had doubts a jury would too.

"Tell us what you see," Mary said.

Owen turned to face her and Kira. They'd been meeting every day over the past week to conduct final witness interviews and shore up their strategy for trial, and she could tell they were both getting frustrated at her insistence they keep digging deeper rather than plunge ahead, full force, with the prevailing theory of a home invasion gone wrong.

"The commissioner's house has a high-tech alarm system, but it wasn't on that night. Fuentes, an admitted burglar, has never been charged with anything related to a gun offense, but on this particular night, he happens to be carrying a Glock G40, and he shoots Mrs. Adams three times. Not enough simply to injure a woman who surprised him in the commission of a burglary, but enough to make certain she would die."

"Does it matter?" Kira said. "Fuentes is going away for life whether he entered with the intent to kill Mrs. Adams or whether he killed her to keep her from screaming. What are you trying to prove?"

"It's not about what I'm trying to prove," Owen said, trying really hard to keep the extra bit of frustration out of her voice. "It's about what Fuentes's attorney will be trying to prove. Ramsey is smart. He's going to point to the lack of motive to try and raise reasonable doubt. He'll say it's not reasonable to believe that Fuentes, a guy with no record of violent crimes, would suddenly become a killer. He'll point out no one saw him pull the trigger, and that it's more likely someone with an actual motive committed the crime."

"Good luck with that," Kira said. "Every angle has been explored."

"Has it?" Owen looked at Mary. "Are you confident there won't be any surprises?"

Mary pushed back from the table and rested her swollen feet on the chair next to her. "Yes, but it never hurts to go through it all again. Commissioner Adams will be here in a little over an hour. Let's make a list of questions and make sure we cover the entire list while he's here. If there are any holes after we talk to him, then we'll make another list and talk to whoever we need to." She turned to Kira. "Sound good to you?"

"It sounds like overkill, but it's not my call." Kira walked toward the door. "I have to make a call. I'll be right back."

When she cleared the door and it shut behind her, Mary gave a low whistle. "Trouble in paradise."

"What's that supposed to mean?" Owen asked.

"It means neither one of you is very good at hiding the tension between you. What happened? Did you stand her up for a big date?"

Owen bristled at the implication. "We aren't dating. Not at all. Not one date."

"Fine, but you are sleeping together. You want to tell me I'm wrong about that?"

Owen didn't want to lie, but she didn't want to talk about it either, and Mary wasn't the type to leave things hanging, unresolved. Owen trusted her to keep a secret more than she trusted her to let things be if she didn't provide some answers. "We aren't. We did, but not anymore. It was nothing. A few times, post happy hour. Didn't mean a thing."

"To you."

"To her too." Even as she spoke the words, Owen questioned their truth. "That's what she said anyway."

Mary rolled her eyes. "And here I thought you were good at picking juries because you're observant, but it turns out you are as clueless as they come. Anyone with eyes can tell Kira's had a thing for you since she started working here."

Owen sank into the chair across from Mary and rubbed her temples. "I've been clear with her from the start."

"It's not working. People hear what they want to hear. Look, I know how hard it is to meet someone when you eat, breathe, and sleep here. Why do you think I married Jack?" she said, referring to her husband who worked in the organized crime unit. "You can sleep with anyone in the building, but you have to consider the fallout first."

"You're saying I have to be willing to marry them if I want to sleep with them?"

"Or suffer the breakup of your working relationship. Kira's one of the best investigators we have. You can request someone else from the pool, but it's your loss if you wind up not getting to work with her because you can't find a good lay elsewhere."

Mary was right. She couldn't undo the harm that had been done so far, but she could try to mend whatever hurt feelings Kira had at being rebuffed. "I'll go talk to her. Straighten things out." She stood and walked to the door.

"If you see a hamburger floating around out there, bring

it back to me. I'm starving." She mimed putting food in her mouth. "And fries. Rescue them from someone skinny who won't appreciate them like I will."

"On it." Owen pulled open the door, determined to find Kira and settle things between them, but she'd barely made it two steps into the hallway before she heard someone call her name. She turned toward the sound and spotted Mia at the opposite end of the hallway, likely coming by to get a status update. Resigned to the fact she'd have to have her talk with Kira later, she started walking in Mia's direction. "Hi, I was headed downstairs to get Mary something to eat. Care to join me?"

Instead of answering, Mia stepped to the side and motioned to someone behind her. A second later, Summer Byrne appeared, and Owen stood in place while her brain cycled through all the possibilities of why Summer was here, at the courthouse, steps from her war room, but she didn't have time to fully process her reaction before Mia and Summer were standing directly in front of her. She plastered a smile on her face and met Summer's eyes. She didn't look like she really wanted to be there. Or maybe Summer simply didn't want to see her again? Owen hoped it wasn't her and then immediately dismissed the thought as inappropriate. Maybe she did have a problem with boundaries after all.

"Owen, I believe you've met Summer Byrne," Mia said, looking between them with a curious expression. "Summer has graciously agreed to work with us on the Adams case. Perhaps you can include her in your meeting with the commissioner this afternoon. Summer understands her role will be described as jury consultant."

Owen tore her gaze from Summer and faced her boss. She wasn't fooled. The whole "perhaps you can include her" was code for "I insist you include her." Fine. She could be a team player even if she didn't get to pick the members of the team. "Looking forward to working with you, Ms. Byrne."

Summer smiled. "Please, call me Summer. And if it's the same to the two of you, I'd prefer to use my grandmother's surname, Harvey, for professional reasons."

Owen nodded, making a note to explore Summer's reasoning further. There was backstory here, and she was determined to find out what baggage Summer was carrying and how it might affect this case. "Harvey. Got it." She looked at Mia. "Will you be joining us for the meeting with Commissioner Adams?"

"I'll stop by but just to say hello. It's your show, Owen. I trust you to do whatever needs to be done." She started walking away. "See you at two."

Except for deciding I need a mind reader as backup. Owen kept a smile plastered on her face until Mia was out of sight.

"I know you don't want me here," Summer said.

Owen avoided her eyes as if she could keep her thoughts private if Summer couldn't see her face, but then that was only buying into the whole mind-reading thing. "Very astute. Did they teach you that in psychic school?"

"Yes."

"What?" Owen stared right at Summer, captivated by the intense blue of her eyes.

Summer broke into a broad smile. "Uh, I'm kidding. There is no psychic school. At least not one I'm aware of. Lord knows I might be better at it if there was one."

An intern approached from the other end of the hallway, and Owen was suddenly conscious that if they stayed there, they were in danger of being overheard. They could duck into the war room, but Mary was in there and Owen wanted a few minutes alone with Summer to lay down some ground rules before she involved her in the case. "Are you hungry?"

"That's a non sequitur for sure, but yes, I'm always hungry."

"I was on my way to the cafeteria to get Mary, my trial partner, a hamburger. Come with?"

"Sure, but you must not like Mary very much if you're feeding her from that place in the basement. I had a sandwich from there last week and it was wretched."

"Probably because no one orders sandwiches there. The one you had was probably a week old. You just don't know how to order."

"And you do? Nan thinks you never eat."

"Nan's right for the most part, but when I do eat, I do it right. Come on, I'll show you." Owen led the way down the stairs to the small cafeteria on the first floor, which was really the basement. When they entered, she walked directly to a counter to the left manned by a tall, skinny man wearing a white paper hat. "Hi, Gerald, how are you doing today?"

"Doing well, Miss O. How about yourself?"

"Can't complain."

"Would you like your usual?"

"Not today. I've brought a guest and I need to show her the best the cafeteria has to offer because she's going to be working with us for a while. Plus, Mary's starving and you know how that can go."

He tsked. "I've seen it firsthand. How about three specials? Here or to go?"

Owen turned to Summer. "Any allergies, dietary restrictions we should know about?"

"Not a one."

"Excellent. Gerald, make that three specials to go, please." She placed a hand on Summer's elbow and steered her to the side of the counter, once again experiencing a hum of energy at the touch. "Sorry, it gets pretty crowded in here."

"You don't have to apologize for keeping me from getting trampled," Summer said. Her eyes narrowed. "Frankly, I'm a little confused by this whole experience. You're feeding me some special, albeit mysterious food and being gallant about the whole experience. I thought you didn't want me here."

"Just because I don't believe in what you do, doesn't automatically make me a jerk. Besides, I kind of owe you a meal. I'm still thinking about that pot roast."

"That's sweet, but it was deceptively simple to make."

"Says you. The only thing I use in my kitchen is a coffee maker, and even that can be a challenge at times."

"I'm thinking you have other talents."

Was Summer flirting with her? Owen thought she had a good instinct for reading people—it was one of her superpowers—but she was having a hard time pinning down any particular vibe from Summer. She didn't have time to try because Gerald called out her name. She collected the food, paid the cashier, and led the way back upstairs, determined she had imagined any flirting.

Mary greeted them at the door with open arms. "Gimme, gimme," she said. When Owen set the three Styrofoam boxes on the table, Mary looked up at her with fluttering eyelashes. "What are you going to eat?"

"Your fries, of course." Owen motioned to Summer, who was still standing in the doorway. "Mary, this is Summer Byrne, sorry, Harvey, the uh, consultant who'll be working with us. You remember, I told you about her," she said, hoping Mary wouldn't blurt out that she'd mentioned she was relieved

Summer had turned her down. "And I hate to break this to you, but one of those is hers."

Mary made a show of clutching the boxes before she grinned and handed one to Summer. "Guard your French fries." She pointed at Owen. "That one will eat them all before you can blink. Trust me, I speak from experience."

"Good to know," Summer said. "I'll guard them with my life."

Owen rolled her eyes and plucked a handful of fries from one of the boxes she'd set in front of Mary.

"Is that really all you're going to eat?" Summer asked.

"That's all she ever eats," Mary answered for her.

"Well—"

"Not true," Owen interrupted before Summer could rat her out about the large helping of pot roast she'd eaten at Summer's house. She wasn't sure why, but she didn't want Mary to know she'd joined Summer's family for dinner. She filed away her reaction to study later and changed the subject. "I'm merely trying to help out since Mary is eating for two."

"Congratulations," Summer said. "When's your due date?"

"Any moment, I hope." She patted her stomach. "Seriously, four weeks from now, but I won't object if we get an early arrival."

"Boy?"

"Are you telling or asking?" At Summer's confused look, Mary pressed on. "I mean, I'd expect a psychic to know the answer."

"Educated guess, based on how low the baby is sitting." Summer reached for her burger and took a bite and groaned. "This is amazing. If I worked here, I would eat this every day."

"Word," Mary said, holding up her free hand for a high five, which Summer met with a clap.

Owen watched the two of them and, for a moment, considered it might be fun having Summer on the team. She hoped she wouldn't be wrong.

CHAPTER TEN

Summer listened to Mary and Owen outline the major points in the case, taking her through the key evidence on the whiteboard, and she began to wonder what she was doing here. The charge was simple, felony murder. Art Fuentes had committed the crime of burglary by breaking into Commissioner Adams's house and killing Mrs. Adams while he was there. Fuentes hadn't said a word since his arrest and he had no known ties to the Adams family or to the commissioner's court, the upshot being there was no underlying motive for the killing other than Mrs. Adams had surprised him and he'd killed her to keep her from being able to ID him. If Joule hadn't been out walking his dog that night and observed Fuentes running from the back door, he might've escaped undetected. With Joule's testimony, the guilt-innocence part of the case was open-and-shut, and with Fuentes's record, a jury would likely have no problem sending him away for a very long time. The facts were straightforward, and Summer couldn't help but think her presence here seemed superfluous.

"Anything stand out to you?" Owen asked.

Summer pursed her lips like she was thinking really hard, but she didn't have much to add. "You said they found the murder weapon, the gun, outside the house. Were there any prints?"

"How do you not already know?" a voice from behind her said. The three of them turned toward the door to see Kira, Owen's investigator, walk into the room. "Shouldn't we be asking you the questions? Or do we even need to ask since you can probably already tell us what we want to know. I mean, isn't that what a mind-reader does?"

"Ease up, Kira," Owen said, flashing her a stern look. "We're going through the evidence with Summer. She's going to be working with us for the duration of the trial." *Whether we like it or not.*

Summer smiled and stuck out her hand. Kira stared at it for a moment before gripping it hard, like she was trying to establish her dominance. "Looking forward to working with you," Summer lied. "And I'm a psychic medium, not a mind-reader. I get it can be confusing."

"Tell you what I'm not confused about—whatever you have to offer is not admissible in a court of law," Kira said.

"You'd be surprised."

Owen cleared her throat and Summer looked in her direction. "Sorry, I guess we're getting off track."

Mary held up a hand. "Hold up. What exactly is a psychic medium?" She pointed at her chest. "Dying to know here."

Summer glanced at Owen, who nodded for her to answer. "Generally speaking, a medium gets their intel from communications with people who have passed on, and a psychic intuits information from other sources, vibrations and the like. Sometimes, the talents overlap, and sometimes a person has both abilities."

"And you're one of those people?" Kira asked, skeptically.

"Yes. Information is shown to me by spirits of the dead, but also by vibrations from the living."

"'Shown' to you?" Mary asked.

"Good catch," Summer said. "Yes. The messages from spirits usually come in dream sequences and visions. Sometimes I get words if the presence is really strong, but often, I see what amounts to pieces of a puzzle."

"Give me an example."

Summer thought for a moment. "Okay, here's one. I might see the front page of a newspaper as a clue about the date something happened, or the story on the page might have some significance to the message the soul is trying to convey."

"Sounds pretty vague and subject to interpretation," Kira said. "And here I thought you could read minds."

I can read yours, and I can tell you are not happy about me being here. "Mind-reading presumes I'm reaching into people's heads and nosing into what I find there, but my abilities are more about cluing into the unspoken words and feelings being projected by both the living and the dead. Because I'm hyper aware of what's going on subconsciously, I tend to pick up a ton of energy from what people are thinking. If the thoughts are backed by strongly held beliefs or carry a lot of emotion, I can often hear exact phrases." She paused for a moment, wondering if Kira got her implication.

"And you don't think listening to people's thoughts is an invasion of privacy?" Owen asked.

Summer was careful to keep any defensive tone out of her voice. "I suppose it can be. I do my best not to hear things without being invited in, so to speak, but if the communication is really strong, it's hard to ignore. It's not a perfect science."

The room went silent and Summer watched while the rest of the group kept their heads down and tension filled the air. "I suppose this means none of you plan to speak to me again?" she asked, hoping to add some levity to the conversation.

"I don't think we need to," Mary deadpanned. "If I

promise I won't count it as an invasion of privacy, can you tell me what I'm thinking right this instant?"

"Hilarious, Mare," Owen said. "Theatrics aside, let's focus on the evidence we have. If nothing else, Summer can provide us with a fresh point of view."

"Happy to help in whatever capacity you need." Summer studied Owen, appreciating the effort she was making to get past the conflict of their initial encounter even though she clearly didn't share her boss's confidence in her special talents. *She's a good girl. Always does the right thing.* Summer almost shielded her eyes at the glow emanating from Owen's direction. She'd caught glimpses of it before, but this time it had shape, the very fuzzy outline of a person, a woman, her voice a gentle whisper, and Summer instantly knew whoever it was, she cared deeply for Owen. *She always does the right thing, but she doesn't take care of herself. Watch out for her.* The shape floated out from behind Owen and came closer, and Summer raised a hand to touch it, unable to resist the pull. At the exact same time, the sharp, pungent odor of cumin filled the air and an image of a pot of bubbling chili flashed in her mind.

"Summer?"

Owen's voice snapped her back into this plane. "Sorry, what?"

Owen pointed. "You raised your hand." She grinned. "Totally not necessary, but I called your name three times and you didn't respond."

"I can't believe you woke her up," Kira said with a smirk. "She was probably on the verge of solving the case."

Summer lowered her arm, slightly embarrassed and consumed with a craving for a bowl of steaming chili, a fact she decided to keep to herself for now while she contemplated the glowing object she'd seen. She'd detected a strong female energy—someone who knew Owen well. Well enough to know what she liked to eat. She wanted to blurt out what she'd learned, share the story, and see if it resonated with Owen. Mary would probably be amused, but Kira was another story. She could feel the burn of Kira's gaze on her and knew she wasn't welcome here. She had a choice. She could let Kira's attitude bother her or she could face it head-on. "I apologize for zoning out, but it happens sometimes, especially when I'm around new people." She shifted in her chair so she was facing Kira. "I thought the case was solved already. I mean, you're about to put a man away for murder. Do you have doubts?"

Kira folded her arms across her chest. "Not in the least."

"We're open to different perspectives about how we present the case," Owen said in an obvious effort to defuse the conflict. A loud buzz sounded, and Owen reached into her pocket and pulled out her phone. "Hang on just a sec."

She stepped out of the room and the energy shifted. Mary was enthusiastic about the case, but also tired, and who could blame her? Kira, on the other hand, held a deep-seated resentment and it wasn't just because she was here to work with them. No, there was something else simmering underneath the surface of her disdain for Summer's abilities. Summer tried to tune in but gave up quickly when faced with the exhaustion of trying to maneuver her way through the tangle of feelings in Kira's head. Thankfully, Owen reappeared before she had to.

"Change of plans," Owen said. "Commissioner Adams has a meeting he can't reschedule this afternoon, so if we're going to meet with him, we have to go to his office."

Mary groaned. "Jack's picking me up for an OB appointment at four. How would you feel about me staying here and putting together the final touches on the pretrial motions?"

Summer watched Owen's jaw clench, but she didn't sense

Owen was upset with Mary. Was she sorry to be stuck with her for the afternoon?

Kira jangled a set of keys. "Come on, Owen. I'll drive."

Owen shook her head. "That's okay. I think it might be best to have a small group for this session. Summer, can you join me? This'll be a good opportunity for you to meet Adams."

She didn't have to have a gift to feel the icy look Kira shot in her direction. Summer didn't want to get in the middle of the weird power dynamic between Owen and Kira, but she also didn't want to shirk her job on the very first day. If she was going to be of any value at all to this team, she needed to meet the players involved, and who better than the victim's husband? "Absolutely."

She stood and followed Owen out of the room. Kira took an exaggerated step out of her way when she approached. *"This won't last."*

She resisted the urge to look Kira in the eye, to say something to let her know she could hear her thoughts, sensing it would be fuel to the fire. She'd have to find another way to win her over or avoid her altogether. In the meantime, she was about to have some alone time with Owen, and the prospect excited her more than she was willing to let on. Thank God no one else in the room read minds.

Owen drove a fully loaded luxurious BMW sedan, not the kind of car Summer expected a county employee to be able to afford, but it suited her as well as the custom-tailored suits she wore. She looked at her hand to see if she wore a wedding band. She didn't. Summer ran her hand along the buttery smooth leather and rosewood paneling and was startled when Owen spoke.

"Would you believe I saved all my lunch money to buy this?"

It wasn't the first time that Owen had read her thoughts,

and Summer tried not to read too much into the revelation. She walked through life like an open book most of the time, naively thinking if anyone could tune in they wouldn't, but Owen's observations felt more intimate than intrusive. She'd shared this kind of back and forth connection with Nan and Faith, but no one else, and definitely not anyone she was attracted to the way she was to Owen, which made the possibility of some kind of psychic link between them titillating. She started to ask Owen if she felt it too, but when she played the question in her head, she decided she sounded the exact kind of crazy that would send Owen running in the opposite direction. "Everyone deserves to have indulgences."

"It's…" Owen bit her bottom lip and gripped the steering wheel, making the turn toward downtown. She smiled and it looked forced. "What about you? What's your favorite extravagance?"

She wondered what Owen had been about to say. She could feel the sadness in her, but Summer couldn't make out the source. It wasn't her business, anyway. *Focus on what's being said out loud.* "Hmm, good question. I'd have to say spa days. I'm a sucker for a good massage and a facial."

"Interesting choice. I was thinking along the lines of something more material."

"I have nothing against material things, but I've found they don't always measure up to good experiences."

Owen nodded, her expression thoughtful. She pulled into the parking garage near the county building and found a prime spot.

"Before we go in, do you want to discuss what role I should play?" Summer asked. She'd worked with Bruce long enough to be able to take certain liberties when they were talking to witnesses or victim's families, but she didn't want to make assumptions about how Owen would want to handle her presence.

"Good question. I hadn't really thought about it. My preference is that you be as unobtrusive as possible. I'll let Adams know you're consulting with us on the case, but otherwise stay in the background and let me do all of the talking. Okay?"

Owen's admonition was abrupt and cool, and Summer was disappointed at the shift in the mood between them, but she couldn't fault her. They were here to work after all.

Commissioner Adams's secretary told them Adams was in a conference with the mayor and invited them to wait in his office. While Owen pretended to be absorbed in her notes, Summer looked around the room, taking in every detail she could about the commissioner's public life. The walls were lined with photos of him shaking hands with presumably local celebrities or engaged in humanitarian enterprises like Habitat for Humanity or handing out food to the homeless. She'd googled the commissioner and familiarized herself with his reputation and exactly what he did. Each county in the state had five county commissioners, one of whom also served as the county judge who was elected county-wide and was essentially the CEO who was in charge of all county business. Each commissioner position was endowed with a lot of authority, but the county judge was in a position of unparalleled power. Prevailing opinion was that the current county judge, Baxter, was planning to retire before the end of the year and Adams, popular not just with his constituents but with the entire electorate, was the predicted successor to fill his spot. Morbid pundits also speculated on whether his wife's murder had made him even more sympathetic as a candidate, and when she'd read those opinions, Summer had felt a tinge of anger on his behalf, but she couldn't identify why.

Loud voices interrupted Summer's thoughts and she looked at the door. Owen pointed at the wall. "I think it's coming from there," she said. "Conference room."

Both of them stared at the wall as the tone escalated on the other side.

"Do I need to remind you what's at stake here?"

"No one knows better than me. But you better tell your friends to steer clear. At some point, there won't be anything left for me to lose."

"You need to think about the rest of your family and your future. Remember, I hear everything."

Summer closed her eyes, trying to sort out the contentious conversation, but other than the strong feeling it was important, she gleaned nothing. When she opened her eyes, Owen was staring at her with a puzzled look.

"What are you doing?"

"Nothing," Summer said, which was mostly true since she couldn't quite identify why what she'd just heard was so important, but she knew that it was. In the interest of being completely honest, she added, "Listening, same as you."

"He and the mayor have a reputation for butting heads, but when it comes to significant issues, they almost always align. I figure we're hearing the butting heads part. They've been at odds about a new development along the Trinity River. Both of them want the development, but they have different ideas about the parameters of the project."

"Makes sense," Summer said, but it didn't really. To an outsider, the two men sounded like they were ready to tear each other's throats out. And the reference to family was very personal. Not at all what she'd expect from a business dispute. If that was how they worked things out in local government around here, she would hate to see how they acted when they truly disagreed over something.

The door swung open and a tall, handsome, dark-haired man strode into the room. "Sorry to keep you waiting." He shook Owen's hand and turned to Summer. He was smiling. Completely at odds with the growling voice she'd heard a moment ago, but it was the kind of smile politicians used to assure voters—big and broad, showing some teeth, but not enough to make you think he wasn't a serious person. "Keith Adams, nice to meet you." He furrowed his brow. "I feel like we've met before. Last month. The fundraiser for Judge Milar at Sammy's?"

She matched his welcoming demeanor with an out-stretched hand. "Afraid not. I'm fairly new to Dallas. Summer Harvey," she answered, remembering at the last minute to use her grandmother's last name.

He grasped her hand and her knees buckled. She struggled to remain upright, but the weight of his touch was leaden, and she could barely keep her hand steady. She started to apologize for her reaction, but before she could form the words, a hazy yellow light swept around his head and pulled her attention into its vortex.

"He's lost."

Summer stared above his head as the light danced and played, casting shadows that ebbed and flowed. *What do you mean?*

"Bring him back."

From where?

"Dig deeper." The voice repeated the command with a whisper in her ear and the warmth of the close voice breathing in her ear sent a shiver down her spine.

"Are you okay?" Adams said, grasping her arm. "You look pale." He led her to the couch. "Here, have a seat."

The moment he let her arm go, the golden hue faded, and the voice was gone, and she scrambled for an excuse to explain away her behavior. "I apologize. I'm feeling a little light-headed."

"Let me get you some water." He walked across the room and opened a mini fridge. "Or maybe you'd prefer a seltzer."

"Water's fine." Summer took advantage of his back being turned to catch Owen's eyes. She was standing across the room watching her with a wary expression. Summer mouthed, "Sorry," and Owen rolled her eyes, clearly exasperated that Summer had done the exact opposite of what she'd asked by drawing attention to herself. When Adams returned with the bottle of water, she held it first against her head, determined to stay in the moment. "Thank you. I'm feeling better already."

"Good." Adams sat on the couch opposite her and invited Owen to join them. "Tell me what I can do for you."

Owen shot her a look that said please don't speak, before responding to Adams. "The trial starts on Monday. Defense counsel hasn't made any overtures about plea deals and, at your request, we haven't made any offers, so we're going forward. Jury selection should take most of the first day and we'll either have opening statements late in the day or the following morning. I know we've gone over your testimony, but I wanted to review the major points and see if you have any questions about areas the defendant's attorney may cover in his cross-examination of you."

"I'll be ready."

"It doesn't hurt to prepare."

He fixed Owen with a hard stare. "I'm not scared if that's what you think."

"I think anyone who lost a loved one and has to come face-to-face with the killer has a right to be a little bit scared. It's healthy and authentic and expected."

Summer got what Owen was saying—the jury would expect to see emotion from him, not the everything's okay, charismatic persona he projected for his electorate. The question was whether he got it as well. "Tell us about your wife," she said, ignoring Owen's stare as she broke the rules she'd laid out.

"Like what do you want to know?"

He didn't meet her eyes and Summer took a moment before responding, leaving space for the voice she'd heard moments ago to interject, but after a few silent seconds, she got nothing. Her intuition told her it had been his wife speaking to her, but if it was, she must've left this space. *It's you, isn't it? Tell me what's on your mind.* She waited a few more seconds and when she didn't get an answer, she pressed on. "What was she like? What did you like best about her? These are the kind of things Owen may ask you about on the stand that will show the jury she's not just another homicide statistic, but a real person whose life has been cut short from unnecessary violence. Anecdotes you can provide will give them focus on putting Fuentes in prison for the rest of his life. Isn't that what you want?"

"Of course," he said, bristling at the question. "She was a loving mother and wife. She used to teach, but when I took this job, she wanted to be home more to take care of things around the house since I was taking on more. She was active in our church and served on the boards of several charities."

The answers were rote and devoid of emotion, but Summer sensed his reticence to give more detail was more about shielding his own feelings than not having any. The main thing she noticed was that he still didn't meet her eyes. *Guilt.* It weighed him down, but it was clouded by something else, something she couldn't quite pinpoint. It might be as simple as he hadn't been home that fateful night to protect her from harm. Or perhaps he had something to do with her death? But if he had, why would his wife be concerned about him?

Summer filed her thoughts away to examine later, but she didn't press him further. Whatever the source of his guilt, he was punishing himself enough about it and there was no need for her to pile on. She reached for his hand and held it and was a bit surprised when he didn't pull away. "I'm sure she loved all of those things, but I'm also sure she loved you more."

Adams squeezed her hand and murmured "Thank you. I didn't deserve it."

Did the statement come from a place of guilt from being alive when his wife wasn't or was there a deeper meaning? Summer looked across the room and met Owen's eyes. She'd half expected Owen to look angry that she'd basically taken over the interview, but instead she looked thoughtful. Summer listened through the silence, both wanting to hear Owen's thoughts and resisting the invasion of privacy. One word came through and Summer heard it loud and clear. *"Respect."*

CHAPTER ELEVEN

Owen pulled out of the parking space and made a left out of the parking garage. Big, fat raindrops spattered the windshield, and the roar of the just brewed storm accurately reflected the tempest raging in her head after watching Summer handle Adams like a skilled therapist guiding her patient to an emotional breakthrough. Summer hadn't said a word since they'd walked out of Adams's office and she seemed weighted down by the visit, but Owen felt the need to say something to cut through the heavy silence in the car. "Good thing Mary didn't come, she would've missed her doctor's appointment for sure."

"Uh-huh." Summer's phone buzzed and she looked at the screen. "Crap."

"What is it?"

"Nan texted me to say she got stuck at her doctor's office. She wants to know if I could pick up Faith from school."

She started texting on her phone at a furious pace. "What are you telling her?" Owen asked.

"I'm texting Faith to let her know I'm downtown without my car and to see if she can hang out inside until I get there."

"Which school? Spence? Long?" Those were the only two names Owen could conjure up.

"Spence."

Owen made an illegal U-turn at the next intersection and stepped on the gas, heading east instead of back to the courthouse. "Tell her we'll be there in less than ten minutes."

"It's okay. She can wait. Besides, I'll still have to get my car from the courthouse."

"I'll take you back after we pick up Faith."

"Seriously, Owen, she'll be fine."

Owen wasn't sure how to read Summer's resistance. Was she merely being polite or did she really not want to be stuck in the car with her? All she knew was she wasn't ready to part ways. *Try one more time and then drop it.* "It's no bother, really. It's a tiny detour. Okay?"

Summer hesitated for a moment and then gave her a reluctant smile. "Okay. You're very sweet, you know."

"Sweet?" Sweet wasn't a word she was used to hearing. Dedicated, loyal, hard-working, but sweet?

"Yes, sweet. No wonder Nan has a crush on you."

Owen warmed to the compliment and she smiled. "Is that so? Is she available?"

"Are you?" Summer's eyes widened and her hand flew to her mouth. "Oh wow, that was inappropriate."

Owen laughed. "Are you asking for Nan or are you asking for you?"

Summer blushed. "I'm sorry. It's none of my business."

"Okay." Owen snuck a look at Summer, who'd slunk down in her seat, and then she took the ramp off the highway and used the time on the service road to toss around the pros and cons of sharing personal information with a virtual stranger, a work acquaintance. But Summer didn't feel like either of those things. She'd been in Summer's home and shared a meal with her family, so they weren't strangers, and Summer tagging along on her case at Mia's request hardly felt like a working relationship. Now they were here in the car together, headed to pick up Summer's daughter from school. She didn't know what words would best define the relationship between them, but oddly enough, accompanying Summer on this family errand was more intimate than anything else she'd shared with anyone in a long time, which likely explained why, when she pulled to a stop at the light ahead, she turned to Summer and said, "I am single, by the way."

Summer turned in her seat and looked at her with a hint of a smile at the corner of her lips. "Duly noted."

"And you?" Owen ventured, injecting a nonchalance she didn't feel into her voice.

"Am I single? Yes, very."

The light changed, leaving Owen no time to check out Summer's expression, but the tone was enough to convey Summer was firmly settled in her single status. Still, Owen couldn't resist another question. "What about Faith's dad? Is he involved in her life?"

"Faith's dad was a one-night stand after a late night party my senior year at Berkeley. My girlfriend and I had broken up the week before and I was exploring my bi side. Turns out I chose a poor specimen to experiment with since when I told him I was pregnant, he didn't believe it could be his. I offered to get a paternity test, but he wasn't interested in having a kid at that stage in his life and I wasn't particularly interested in tying myself and my unborn child to a guy who'd turned out to be kind of a jerk."

"Makes perfect sense. So, you had Faith on your own."

"Completely. I barely knew Nan then—she and my mother never really got along. And when my parents found out I'd gotten pregnant, they had a lot of opinions, most of which involved me going into seclusion for the duration of my pregnancy and giving my baby up for adoption. When I told them I wasn't interested in their plan, they cut me off. Without their help and with a new baby to raise, I wound up deferring my admission to Hastings Law."

"You went to law school?"

"I was supposed to. That was the goal, anyway. Law school, then a job with the ACLU or NCLR or the Southern Poverty Law Center." She grinned. "I was very idealistic and very much all about resisting authority." Her expression became serious again. "Raising a baby on my own was harder than I thought, and I kept putting off law school. Relationships were hard because people say they're fine with a ready-made family, but when you have to interrupt a date to go home because the babysitter calls to tell you your kid is throwing up or your kid wanders into the bedroom wanting you to read her one more story while you're trying to be intimate, you pretty quickly find out someone's staying power. Couple that with the visits from dead people in the middle of the night and the dating pool shrinks even further, so I focused on making the best life I could with just the two of us."

"So, with law school out of the picture, you decided to put your 'gift' to use?" Owen tried not to stumble over the word, but she could hear the slight edge in her voice when she echoed the term Summer had used for her supposed psychic skills.

"Oh, I was all about ignoring the gift at first. I took a job as a paralegal for a local firm. One thing led to another, and I wound up helping out the local sheriff on a case, not with any of my paralegal prowess, but by using the abilities I'd spent most of my life trying to squelch. It was a revelation. At first…Anyway, the sheriff gave my name to Bruce, the DA in Santa Cruz, and I worked with Bruce for several years before I decided to move out here."

Owen had a ton more questions, like how Summer had

reconnected with Nan and why exactly she'd left Santa Cruz, and whether she'd been in a relationship when she'd left, and why, if she'd found a calling, she'd been reluctant to use it when Owen had first approached her about working on this case. She settled on the least personal of the topics. "I've only been to Santa Cruz once, but I find it hard to believe anyone would leave there voluntarily."

"I know, right? It's even better to be a local than a visitor because then you get to know all of the offbeat places tourists don't see, and trust me, there are a lot. Faith and I had some good times there."

Before Owen could ask another question, Summer pointed at the building up ahead on the right. "She's usually waiting over there. Yep, I see her."

Owen steered the car toward the driveway, and when she drew in closer, she motioned for Summer to lower the window. Summer called out to Faith, but Faith stood in place, squinting at them for a full minute before she appeared to recognize her mom in a strange car. Once she did, though, she jogged toward them and leaned down to look in the window.

"Hey, Owen."

"Hey, Faith. I'm your chauffeur if that's okay."

Faith exchanged a look with her mom and burst into a broad grin. "Better than okay," she said as she reached for the door handle and climbed inside. Once she was settled in, she leaned forward into the console space. "What's the plan?"

"Owen is taking me, us, back to the courthouse where my car is parked and then you and I will head home. You'll do homework, while I prep dinner. I'm thinking chili. Thoughts?"

"Sounds fab. Can Owen stay for dinner?"

"Honey, Owen probably has work to do. She brought me to pick you up as a favor, but she's a very busy person. Maybe another time."

Owen replayed the words, searching for clues about whether Summer really didn't want her to stay for dinner or whether she was simply teaching Faith boundaries, while she hoped Summer would join in Faith's request.

"But Nan says she needs to eat more. Owen, what will you eat if you go home by yourself?"

"Faith," Summer said in a low growl. "You're being a busybody."

Owen laughed. "It's okay. Don't worry, Faith. I have a freezer full of perfectly balanced dinners. All I have to do is pop one in the microwave and I'm all set."

Faith stuck out her tongue and made a gagging sound. "See, Mom?"

Summer raised her hands in surrender. "Owen, would you like to join us for dinner?"

Owen paused for a moment to assess whether Summer was only inviting her because she'd been pressured by Faith before deciding Summer didn't seem like the kind of person who let herself be pushed into doing something she didn't want to do. Besides, the invitation sounded sincere and she could think of nothing she'd rather do. "Believe it or not, chili is my absolute favorite dish. I'd love to."

❖

"What time did you tell her to come over?" Nan asked.

"Six thirty. Faith has a big test tomorrow and I don't want her staying up too late." Summer ran a knife along the edge of the red onion, discarded the skin in the trash, and chopped what remained into thick chunks. When she was done, she scanned the kitchen counter. The chili was simmering in a pot on the stove and the counter was lined with bowls of the rest of their favorite toppings—sharp cheddar cheese, sour cream, jalapeños. Before she'd started her homework, Faith had grated the cheese, barely able to contain her excitement at having company for the second time in as many weeks. Summer made a mental note they needed to be more social, no matter how naturally resistant she was to expose their little family to other people. Why did time with Owen not feel like an invasion?

"Are you going to change?" Nan asked in a tone that said "please do."

Summer looked down at her outfit. She'd switched her suit for joggers, an ancient Berkeley T-shirt, and her favorite Reefs—perfect clothes for cooking but not so much for having guests. She'd fully intended to change before Owen arrived, but she decided to tease Nan for a moment. "What's wrong with what I'm wearing?"

Nan twisted the dishtowel in her hand and snapped it at her in a playful move. "You're hilarious. Go put on something presentable. But don't wear that formal stuff you wear to court. I'm thinking casual but flirty. Git. I'll set the table."

Summer ducked out of the path of the snapping towel and jogged upstairs. She'd worn her favorite pantsuit to the courthouse this morning, a vestige of her former life. Hosting Owen for a home-cooked dinner definitely merited a more casual look, but after years of only sporadic dating, flirty wasn't in her repertoire. Which was fine, because tonight wasn't about flirting. The only reason Owen was joining them for dinner was because Faith had begged and Summer was powerless to resist granting her daughter such small favors when she knew Faith was having trouble fitting in at a new school where everyone was a stranger. *Like you aren't a little bit excited that Owen is coming over tonight.*

She pushed her inner voice aside and combed through the hangers in her closet, finally settling on an indigo blue sweater, faded blue jeans, and her favorite pair of Frye boots. She held the sweater up to her neck and looked at her reflection in the mirror. The saleslady had commented about how the color accentuated her blue eyes, but she'd bought it for the flattering scoop neckline. She vividly remembered the day she'd made the purchase. She'd gone shopping for something new to wear for a first date. A first date that hadn't happened because that morning the story broke that she'd been assisting the Santa Cruz DA's office and her special skills had missed the mark. The date had ghosted her, never showing up, never calling or texting, and Summer was certain the brush-off was a direct result of the publicity. She'd seen her picture reflected everywhere she went. People pointed in public, Faith got harassed at school, and the one safe place Summer had carved out for them in the world no longer felt safe. She quit her job and holed up in their apartment until one night, her grandfather, Charlie, had come to her in a dream and told her to call Nan. Two weeks later, she and Faith arrived in Dallas to start their new life.

In the flurry of the move and settling in, there'd been no time to think about dating, and she'd been fine with that. Tonight wasn't a date, but she was going to wear the sweater anyway because it made her feel good and confident and like a boss, and up against Owen's strong energy, she needed all the help she could get. She peeled off her T-shirt, slipped on the sweater, touched up her makeup, and took a step back to assess the result in the full-length mirror. Happy with what she saw, she dabbed on some of her favorite cologne and walked out of her room where she ran into Faith in the hallway.

"Homework's all done. Do you need me to set the table?"

"Pretty sure Nan's got that covered." Summer looked her up and down, noting the new pink Chucks she'd been saving for a special occasion. "You changed clothes."

"You did too."

"True."

"We're having company," Faith said. "We haven't had company since we've been here. Well, except for last week when Owen was here, but that was different because that time we didn't invite her in advance. Right?"

"Uh, right." Summer took a minute to process Faith's excitement. She didn't want to squelch it, but she wanted to set realistic expectations. "She's definitely invited this time, but it's still a work thing. And it's temporary. The trial starts in a few days and it will probably last two weeks tops. Then it's back to looking for a job for me, and Owen will be working on other cases."

Disappointment flashed in Faith's eyes, but it was quickly replaced with the bright light of a new idea. "Maybe you can get a job working at her office?"

The doorbell rang, saving her from having this particular conversation. Faith took the stairs two at a time and threw open the front door. Summer heard her greet Owen with as much enthusiasm as she'd ever seen her have about anything, and she vowed not to do anything to squelch it. She'd work this case with Owen and when it was over, if she never saw her again, she'd deal with the fallout if Faith was disappointed. And as for her own disappointment? She'd have to find a way to deal with that too.

"Mom, Owen's here."

Summer paused on the landing and watched as Owen and Faith engaged in a lively conversation about Faith's school. Owen wore dark jeans, black loafers, and a fitted lux-looking black V-neck sweater. Cashmere, maybe? She'd have to feel it to be sure, and suddenly the idea of running her hands along Owen's side sent a warm flash through her entire body. It had been too long since she'd been intimate with anyone.

Surely that was the reason her body kept reacting the way it did whenever she was around Owen. Whatever the reason, it needed to stop. They were in each other's lives for a temporary purpose and, just like she'd told Faith, when this case was over, they would part ways, each moving on to their different lives. She took a deep breath and descended the stairs.

They both stopped talking as she approached, and Owen handed her a bottle of wine. "I hear this is a good wine to pair with chili, but I realize it's a weeknight, so feel free to stash it for another time."

Summer read the label. Chateau Petrus Pomerol. It looked French and fancy—not exactly chili material, but she decided to go with it. "Let's have a glass." She led the way to the kitchen, but not before noticing Faith slip her hand into Owen's and tug her along. Instinct told her she should do more to discourage Faith's instant bond with Owen, but how could she when she was developing a bond of her own?

While Faith regaled Owen with tales of her science project, she rummaged through the cabinet for proper wine glasses, but all she could come up with were the short juice glasses she used every day, caring more about what was in the glass than how it reached her lips. With the whirlwind her life had become over the past couple of months, drinking straight from the bottle would've been an option if she weren't worried what Faith would think.

"Why aren't you talking to your company?" Nan whispered in her ear.

"Because I'm busy trying to find a wine glass for said company," Summer whispered back, glancing across the room, happy to see Owen, thoroughly engaged in her conversation with Faith. "She brought a bottle and it looks expensive."

Nan reached up and closed the cabinet door. "I keep the good glasses in the hutch in the dining room." Summer started to head that way, but Nan pulled her back. "Go talk to Owen, and I'll get the glasses." She lowered her voice even more. "She looks good in a suit but even better like this. Right?"

Summer rolled her eyes, but Nan was right. Casual Owen was even more delectable than the courtroom litigator version, probably because she seemed more approachable. Summer knew better—Owen was way more vulnerable, even in a suit, than she liked the world to believe, and she wondered what had happened in Owen's life to make her feel like she had to put up barriers between her and the rest of the world.

But tonight wasn't about that. She wasn't sure what tonight was about, but she decided to take it one step at a time and the first step was dinner. She opened the oven door and pulled out a cast iron skillet.

"Is that cornbread?"

Summer nearly dropped the pan in surprise to find Owen standing right behind her. Owen reached out to help her and their hands touched for a brief instant, but enough to send Summer into overdrive. "Sorry," Owen said. "I didn't mean to startle you."

Summer took a deep breath and set the skillet on a trivet, hyperaware Owen was still standing close behind her. "It's okay. And yes, cornbread. It's my fav with chili."

"Mine too."

Owen's eyes closed as she spoke, and Summer caught a glimpse of the aura from earlier, filling the space between them. Owen's mood was heavy and joyful at the same time, and Summer couldn't resist asking, "What are you thinking?"

Seconds trudged by before Owen opened her eyes and grinned, all traces of sadness evaporated. "You mean you don't know?"

Summer rolled her eyes, but inside she yearned for another glimpse of the aura, certain it would give her a glimpse into

Owen's psyche. And she desperately wanted that glimpse. Maybe too much. She shook away the thought and pointed at the bowls on the counter. "I hope you like toppings."

"I do." Owen smiled. "And I see you're a fan of all the right ones."

"Well, I mean my chili's pretty good, but it's merely a palette." Summer grinned. "Toppings are life."

"I'm in complete agreement." Owen pinched a few shreds of cheese, popped them in her mouth, and moaned. "Oh, that's the good stuff."

Summer's stomach flipped at the visceral pleasure Owen displayed. She shut her eyes briefly and imagined feeding Owen bits of cheese, enjoying the soft interplay when she touched Owen's mouth with the tips of her fingers. Would Owen moan at her touch?

Nan appeared with the wine glasses at that moment, saving her from having to contemplate things that would never happen. Things she wasn't even sure she wanted to happen. Being around Owen opened up all of her senses and the ensuing onslaught of sensations was affecting her ability to focus. That was all this was—nothing more. She poured three full glasses of wine and handed one to Nan and one to Owen.

Nan downed a liberal swallow. "This is delicious." She examined the bottle. "I don't recall having seen this brand before."

Owen shrugged. "I pulled it out of my stash at home. I think it might have been a gift."

"Nice gift," Faith called out from the kitchen table where she was holding her cell phone. "It's been sold out for years. The only place someone might get a bottle is from this auction house in France and they give first bidding rights to their wealthy members. You're not a member, are you, Owen?"

Owen laughed. "Not hardly."

"Then you're out of luck, Mom. Guess you'll have to settle for that stuff you buy at the grocery store."

Summer rolled her eyes. "Thanks, Faith. Appreciate the vote of confidence." She took a sip of the wine, followed quickly by another. "Oh wow. This is amazing." She reached for the bottle. "I'm half tempted to hide the rest of this and keep it to myself. Nan?"

Nan took another sip. "Beautiful bouquet," she announced. "Let's skip the chili and have this for dinner."

"I'm with you," Summer said. "Food is overrated."

"Hey," Faith said, waving her hand in their direction. "Remember the twelve-year-old whose idea this whole dinner was. She's hungry, and not for grape juice. Chili's getting cold."

The room was quiet for the next few minutes as they dug into dinner. Summer used the time to think, weighing which topics would be most likely to get Owen to talk without making her feel like she had to discuss the case. In a perfect display of mind reading, Faith beat her to the punch.

"Owen, does your family live in Dallas?"

Summer caught the flicker of sadness in Owen's eyes. It was a quick flash, rapidly replaced by a neutral expression, but she was certain the sadness ran deeper than Owen let on.

"I don't have a lot of family. It's mostly just me. But I've lived here most of my life. Bring on all your Dallas questions and I promise I can find you answers."

Faith opened her mouth and, afraid she was going to pry, Summer summoned all the energy she could muster. *"Let's not ask her a lot of questions. She'll share things about herself as we get to know her."* Faith flashed her a smile to signal she'd gotten the message, and then plunged into a mini interrogation about the best museums in town. Summer breathed a sigh of relief, but there was a part of her that was disappointed because she wanted to know everything she could about this enigmatic woman, but she didn't want to do it in front of Faith and Nan. *I need to find a way to get some private time with her*. She met Owen's eyes and was startled at the feeling that Owen was seeing into her head, reading her thoughts. As it had earlier, the idea of sharing a psychic connection with another person, especially a smart, attractive woman like Owen was exciting, but she realized she was probably just projecting. On the off-chance Owen was really able to see into her head, she boldly unfurled the one message that dominated her thoughts at this very moment. *I wish we were alone right now.*

Owen cleared her throat and the connection was broken. "When this trial is over," she said to Faith, "I'll take you, and your mom and Nan, of course, to the Perot Museum of Natural History. It's fascinating and I'm a member so I get to bring guests for free." She turned to Summer. "In the meantime, we have some trial prep to do. Are you free tomorrow night? I know it's a Friday, but it tends to be the quietest time of the week for me."

"Absolutely," Summer said, acutely conscious of Faith and Nan mentally cheering her on. *"It's work, you two."* "I'm at your disposal for the duration of the trial."

"Good to know."

Owen held her gaze for a moment and everything else receded. After a few seconds, Summer felt compelled to change the subject because they weren't alone and this wasn't private. Tomorrow. Tomorrow she could be alone with Owen and have a better shot at examining these feelings without an audience. She pointed at Owen's bowl. "You left some."

Owen looked down at her bowl. "I didn't mean to." She

ate the last bite and scraped her spoon around the inside of the bowl like a kid wishing for a second helping of ice cream.

"There's plenty more."

Owen grinned. "That obvious?"

"Pretty much." Summer reached out a hand, motioning for Owen to hand her the bowl. The spell between them was broken, but this sharing of the everyday was nice too. "I'm glad you like it."

"Like it?" Owen shook her head. "Love it is more accurate." She patted her stomach. "But I better not have any more or I won't be able to walk out of here."

"We'll pack you a to-go box," Faith said. "Right, Mom?"

"Great idea," Summer said. "Cornbread too?"

"That would be amazing." Owen set her napkin on the table and leaned back in her chair. "This was the perfect dinner. Lucky for me you invited me over when you were making my favorite meal."

Summer watched Nan and Faith exchange grins, and she raised her napkin to her lips to hide her own, but it was too late. Owen narrowed her eyes. "What's going on?"

Faith pointed at the empty dish. "Not a coincidence."

Owen looked at Nan, who nodded in confirmation. "Nope," Nan said.

When Owen finally turned to her with a question in her eyes, Summer raised her hands in surrender. "Guilty as charged. I got a hint about the chili and I went with it. I promise I wasn't reading your mind." She wasn't lying since it was the spirit surrounding Owen who gave her the message, not Owen herself. Summer waffled about saying anything else before she decided to wade slowly into the subject. "Was it your mom who used to make it for you?"

The minute the words landed, she wished she could reel

them back in. Owen's friendly demeanor shuttered closed and she clenched her hands in her lap. "I'm sorry. That's none of my business."

"It's okay," Owen said, her voice on the edge of curt, belying the words. "You know, I should get going. I have a lot of trial prep to do still. Dinner was amazing and I truly appreciate you having me over." She edged her chair back and it scraped against the floor making a loud awkward squeak.

Summer ignored Faith's pleading expression and her silent voice, begging her to stop Owen. She was as disappointed at Owen's change in mood as Faith, but she couldn't blame Owen for wanting to protect herself from being vulnerable. It wasn't like she didn't feel exactly the same. When was she going to learn to maintain boundaries between what she knew and what was appropriate to share? She'd put Owen on the spot by bringing up her deceased mother—she was certain that's who had appeared to her—and now she'd ruined their pleasant evening. The least she could do was not make it any more awkward than it already was. She stood and faced Owen across the table, injecting all the compassion she could muster into her gaze. "I'll walk you out."

Owen said polite, but stiff, good nights to Nan and Faith and followed her to the door. Summer put her hand on the doorknob but paused before opening it. "I'm sorry. I had no right to bring up your personal life. It's hard not to share when I get a caring message, and I'm certain whoever it was that told me you liked chili was someone important to you, someone who cared about you very much." She paused, noting the pained look on Owen's face. "And here I am, doing it again."

Owen cracked a hint of a smile and Summer wanted to ask if she would see her tomorrow, if she still wanted her to help prep for trial, or whether she was going to stay mad at her for a very long time, but she also didn't want to fill this heavy space between them with words that didn't have anything to do with the feelings she was having about Owen. Strong feelings. Connected feelings. Feelings that continued to bubble to the surface no matter how much she tried to ignore them, so she embraced them instead, reaching for Owen's hand. Their fingers laced for a moment before Owen released the hold and took a step back.

"I have to go," she said, her voice barely above a whisper.

"I know."

"Thank you."

Owen placed extra emphasis on the words, and Summer wondered about the underlying message. Thank you for dinner? Thank you for not asking more questions? Thank you for not asking me to stay? She couldn't quite home in on which, so she said the only thing that seemed appropriate. "You're welcome."

As she watched Owen walk down the steps to her car, Summer thought of a million better things she could've said. She hoped she'd get the chance.

CHAPTER TWELVE

Owen heard a rattle and looked toward the conference room door for about the sixth time that afternoon, but like all the other times, the sound appeared to come from someone walking by in the hall outside. There was no knock, the door didn't open, and Summer didn't walk through ready to work like last night hadn't happened.

But last night had happened, and even if she couldn't quite define what had gone wrong, she knew something had changed between her and Summer. What had felt like a mild flirtation had suddenly gone deep and intense, and the associated mix of feelings left her both confused and stimulated. She'd contemplated calling Summer several times after she'd left, but every time she stopped before connecting the call, unsure what she would say and even more unsure about what would happen if she opened the door. Because that's what it felt like with Summer. Every time she spoke to her it was like she was inviting Summer to walk through spaces she'd never invited anyone else in. Spaces she wasn't sure she wanted to revisit.

And then there was the connection between them so strong it felt like a bond, bridging thoughts and feelings between them, no words necessary. She'd never experienced anything like it, and she wasn't sure she believed it had actually happened, but in the moment, she would've sworn Summer knew her every thought and vice versa. She'd probably just been high on the wine and the spice of the chili.

The chili. If Summer didn't have any special powers, was the chili dinner and the reference to her mother nothing more than a lucky fortune-teller trick? Ever since leaving Summer's house so abruptly the night before, she'd been mulling over why she'd reacted the way she had. Summer had made her favorite meal—a thoughtful, caring gesture. But Owen had stayed up half the night trying to think of a logical way Summer would've known chili was her comfort food, the one thing she and her parents would make themselves on the night the chef had off. She had vivid memories of her mother measuring out the spices while her dad grated the cheese and cut the onion. They'd load up big bowls and curl up in front of the huge screen in the media room to watch the Dallas Stars or the Mavericks when they were at away games. Her dad would announce that in his opinion watching from home was way better than watching the games from the suites they owned, and fourteen-year-old Owen agreed. She was always bored in the suite, not understanding why people would rather talk business than about the sporting event playing out only yards away. Plus, the fancy food they served was never as good as the chili her mother made.

She tore her gaze from the conference room door back to the whiteboard in the front of the room, and caught Mary staring at her with her eyebrows raised in question. "What?"

"I should be asking you," Mary said. "You keep looking at that door and I can't tell if you're excited or scared of who might walk through." She cocked her head. "I'm getting more of an excited vibe. Speaking of which, where is Kira? Are you and she back on again?"

Owen's stomach clenched. "She's bringing Joule in for

trial prep. And no. Nothing's going on between us. Never again."

"Have you mentioned that to her?"

She hadn't talked to Kira about anything but the case all week, which was her way of letting Kira know they needed to focus on the trial and nothing else. Ironic, considering she'd been having trouble of her own focusing on the trial since Mia insisted she bring Summer on board. But the fractured focus that came from her attraction to Summer was very different from the circumstantial loneliness that had drawn her to Kira. She'd spent most of the time since she'd left Summer's house last night sorting through why, but the only conclusion she'd been able to reach was that both were affecting her work, and she needed to erect a boundary or her work would suffer. "No, but I think she gets the point."

The door rattled again, but Owen resisted looking this time, conscious of Mary's focused attention on her every move. She didn't trust her ability to tamp down her excitement if Summer actually showed up, and she wasn't interested in fielding a bunch of questions from Mary if she figured out why she was so jumpy. She kept her face fixed in what she hoped was a neutral expression and slowly turned to see who was at the door, relieved and disappointed to see Mia's intern, Tad Wiley.

"Ms. Rivera asked me to let you know she'd like an update by end of day." He was gone before either of them could reply.

"Great," Mary said. "Tell her the update is we won't know anything more until we start picking the jury on Monday."

"I'll come up with something to tell her," Owen said. "I'm sure she's getting calls from the press looking for a statement, and Adams is probably bugging her for intel about strategy."

"How did your meeting with him go yesterday? Did Summer get any psychic vibes?"

"She says she did, but nothing specific about the case. It was weird, though. He really gravitated to her, and for the first time since I've known him, I actually felt like he was expressing some genuine emotions and not just the stuff he plays for the crowd to get votes." It was Summer. She brought out the emotion in people. Owen knew it for a fact.

"Interesting. So, are you over the whole he hired someone to kill his wife thing?"

"I'm keeping my options open." She remembered Summer's reaction to the argument Adams had with the mayor. She'd explained it away as professional differences at the time, but had she been too quick to write it off? It was probably nothing. "He had a fight with the mayor. Right as we got to his office. It was heated," she blurted out the words before she changed her mind.

"Okay. Do you think that has something to do with his wife?"

Now Owen felt silly for bringing up the disagreement. She was letting Summer's woo-woo nonsense get in her head. "No, but if anything comes up during the trial to suggest he might've been involved, I'll be leading the charge." She heard the door open again and, assuming it was Tad again, she called out, "I promise I'll update her before the end of the day, but if you keep interrupting, we won't have anything to update her about."

"Guess I picked a bad time to show up."

Owen immediately recognized the soft, light cadence of Summer's voice. "You came." She blurted out the words as she turned to face her, before she could think to filter her thoughts. Totally out of character, but right now, in this moment, she didn't care.

"Of course, I came. I promised, didn't I?"

Owen tore away from the memories flooding her mind

and focused her attention on Summer. She was beautiful inside and out. Owen could feel it with every ounce of her being, and she was so entirely relieved Summer had shown up today after she'd practically run from her the night before. "You did. Thank you."

Mary cleared her throat and they both looked in her direction. Owen wondered if Summer could read Mary's mind in this moment because she was pretty sure Mary was wondering what was going on between them. Owen couldn't answer because she wasn't sure. How would Summer respond if asked the same question?

"Hi, Summer," Mary said. "Glad you could join us."

Summer stepped farther into the room. "Are you sure I'm not interrupting anything?"

"Not at all. Owen and I were just talking about your meeting with Commissioner Adams yesterday. We have a running battle over whether he was involved in his wife's murder. Did you happen to get a read on that?"

"Mary!" Owen stared at her unable to believe she'd shared her private musings about Adams.

Mary hunched her shoulders. "What? She's working with us on the case, right? Seems like she needs to know everything we're thinking if she's going to be helpful."

Summer settled into a chair at the table across from Mary and a few feet from Owen. "She's right. It is helpful if I know of any specific concerns you have. My mind-reading skills are not perfect, after all." She grinned. "Seriously, if you have concerns about my ability to be discreet, don't worry. I've worked closely with law enforcement and the district attorney in Santa Cruz and surrounding counties for years, and while my accuracy may have been called into question, my ethics were never an issue. Whatever you share here stays with me. You have my word."

"I didn't mean to imply you weren't trustworthy," Owen said.

"I know."

A few beats of silence passed during which Owen wished she were alone with Summer so she could properly apologize for rushing off last night. For the first time in her life, she wanted to give another person some context about her life, to explain where she was coming from, and how she'd become who she was, share her secrets and wrest her way out from under them.

"I get you."

Owen heard Summer's voice clearly, but she was certain Summer hadn't spoken the words out loud. She flicked a glance at Mary, whose expression hadn't changed and showed no reaction to Summer's words. She shook her head, unsure if she'd imagined the response, but deciding to accept it as legit, because real or imagined, it was exactly what she needed to hear.

"Do you want to hear my thoughts about Commissioner Adams?" Summer asked.

She wanted to hear lots of things, but none in front of Mary. "Yes," Owen said. "Unvarnished truth. I could tell you had a strong connection with him."

Summer steepled her fingers and closed her eyes for a moment. "We did connect, but not one on one. Despite the fact he appeared to show a lot of emotion toward the end of our visit, he was very walled off. I suppose it could have something to do with whatever he was arguing with the mayor about, but there's a lot going on there, but it's buried deep. Most of what I got was from another presence in the room. Female, very close to the commissioner."

"Mrs. Adams?" Mary asked.

Summer nodded. "Could be. It was definitely someone

who's passed on, so it makes sense that it would be her. I didn't see a recognizable image—mostly light and shadows—but the way she talked about him, it had to be someone close. She said things like he's lost his way and bring him back. Something about digging deeper."

"Well, that's weird," Owen said. "But it doesn't sound exactly like he had anything to do with her dying. Wouldn't she have mentioned it if that were the case?"

"Come on, Owen," Mary said. "Summer already said it doesn't work that way. She gets puzzle pieces and the entire box isn't necessarily on display to give her the big picture."

"True," Summer said. "I wasn't sure what to make of what she said at the time, and part of that was because the encounter was incredibly intense—it left me feeling out of sorts and fuzzy about exactly what she said. Now that I know you have some concerns about whether he was involved in his wife's death, I feel like there's some energy around that, even some guilt, but no blame from her at all, if that makes any sense."

"Not really," Owen said. "Either he was involved or he wasn't. Can you ask her?"

"Sure. We're going to happy hour together later and I'll ask her then."

"Very funny," Owen said. "Okay, I get it. She doesn't show up on command, but maybe there's a way to conjure her up?"

"I can try, but I can't promise anything. These spirits run the show. They are the ones who decide to come forward. It's not like I woke up one day and thought, 'Hey, I think I'll talk to dead people today and see what I can find out about the world.'"

Owen started to ask Summer if she'd always possessed this skill, talent, whatever, but the question felt intimate and she resolved to wait until they were alone. "How about we move on since there's plenty of other stuff to work on. The witness who saw the defendant leaving Adams's house is coming in today. You know, the guy who you saw being strangled." Owen tapped her own head to indicate "saw" meant intuited, and was surprised she didn't feel compelled to roll her eyes at the idea Summer had indeed seen the attack on Joule. When had her perspective shifted and would it affect her ability to sort fact and fiction when it came to the evidence in this case? She shoved the thoughts aside and refocused on their plan for the day. "And we were going over questions for the jury panel and our ideas about the ideal juror for this case. Are you okay sticking around to work with us?"

"Absolutely. Nan and Faith are headed to a movie tonight and I told them I might be late."

Owen's mind wandered to ideas about getting Summer alone. So they could talk. And...whatever else she could conjure up to do with Summer on her own. Right now, her mind was doing a lot of conjuring. She shook her head to do a reset and get back to focusing on the case. "Perfect. While we wait for the witness, let's talk about juries. I figure since you were on one recently, you might have some good insights."

She grinned to let Summer know she'd gotten past the verdict in the Jex case. She hadn't really, but she no longer blamed Summer. If the jury had that many questions about the defendant's guilt, she'd done something wrong during the trial, and better to learn more about that now than when she was in trial on a much bigger case.

"I do have a few things to mention," Summer said, "but you may not want to hear them."

"Try us," Mary said.

"Trying to figure out what you need in a juror in advance is a waste of time."

❖

Summer watched Owen's and Mary's faces and could tell they were gearing up to defend their position. Owen's first words after her conclusive statement left no doubt.

"You think we don't know what we're doing?" Owen asked.

The edge in Owen's voice was undeniable. Summer didn't want to argue with her, but she also didn't want to work on this case if she wasn't able to express her opinions without being dismissed. She summoned the confidence that came from years of reading people more thoroughly than most. "You can't do this in the abstract. You'd be better off just taking the first twelve people on the panel and focusing your efforts on the evidence in the case."

Owen stiffened, and Summer could feel the tension coming off her in waves. Thankfully, Mary spoke first. "Tell us what you mean."

"I've helped pick lots of juries. The benefit of not being one of the trial lawyers is I get to spend more time looking at the case from a lay person's point of view. The most important thing I've learned is that the lawyers about to try the case are way too immersed in the facts and law, and they have a tendency to project that knowledge onto the people on the jury panel." Summer cleared her throat and took a moment to connect with Owen before she continued speaking. *"Don't take this personally."* "Take for example the jury I was on a couple of weeks ago. Remember Wayne?"

Owen rolled her eyes. "Mr. I Just Have One More Thing To Say About That?" She turned to Mary. "Showboat, know-it-all. Very law-and-order."

"Right," Summer said. "I bet you and Ben both thought he

was going to be the jury foreman and that quiet little me was someone you didn't have to worry about at all. Am I right?"

Owen hesitated a second, and Summer could tell she was trying to come up with something to say that didn't make her look like a jerk for thinking Wayne, the guy who fancied himself the lord of all the jurors, was more likely to be voted in as foreman than her.

"Yes, you're right. In my experience," Owen said, "the loudmouths have a tendency to bully their way into power, and a contributing factor is the rest of the jurors aren't interested in taking on the responsibility. Besides, you didn't say a word while you were on the panel."

"True, but you know that's fairly common. And I'm sure as obnoxious as Wayne was during voir dire, you didn't strike him because you thought he was a sure guilty vote. And he was. For the first few rounds, but then his unwillingness to even try to see another side started to turn the rest of the jurors off."

"Or you were simply more persuasive in your defense of the guy with the drugs in his car."

The edge of sarcasm in Owen's voice was expected, but it still riled Summer. "Seriously? I spent the last few years of my life helping convict criminals and send them to prison. Do you really think I suddenly developed an aversion to seeing people who do bad things get punished?"

Mary raised a hand. "How about we all assume we're on the same side until proven otherwise." She shot a look at Owen who nodded slowly. "Okay then. Summer, tell us where you're going with all this."

"Almost everyone can be persuaded. The ones that can't—crime victims, law enforcement personnel—you or defense counsel should be able to identify and strike for cause, but the rest can be won to your side as long as you know what makes them tick and you're willing to tailor your case to fit their worldview in some way. I've observed a lot of trial attorneys, and all of them know their cases better than anyone else, but the jurors only hear the story once. Whatever you say, starting with voir dire, has to resonate with them right away or it won't stick. If it doesn't stick, then they get back in that jury room and they can be swayed to either side. The mistake most lawyers make is they assume jurors approach the case with the same worldview they have, but it's not that simple." Summer stopped talking, concerned she was starting to sound like she knew more than they did about trying cases. "Look, I know you know this stuff, but it's easy to lose perspective when you're in the middle of the process."

"And how do you suggest we accomplish getting in the heads of these jurors right from the start?" Owen asked.

"Start by practice pitching your case to someone who knows nothing about it. Someone whose place in life and/or worldview is very different than your own. Get their feedback. Listen to what they say they heard. Remember, they only get to hear the evidence one time. If the person you're pitching to asks you to repeat what you've said, politely tell them no and watch them struggle to come to a decision. Remember that when you're in court so that you can ensure you make the most of the important points. And listen to what they're not saying."

"Isn't that what you're here for?" Owen asked.

"Sure, but it's a skill you can learn if your mind is quiet and open to hearing."

"Now, you're telling us we should read the jurors' minds and you're going to teach us how?"

Summer laughed. "If only. Then I could collect my paycheck and go home and change into leggings and a baggy T-shirt while you two do battle in court." Owen and Mary didn't join in her laughter. Instead they both just looked puzzled. "I'm no guru with a box full of tricks to tell you how to pick the perfect juror. The best help I can give you is to say that you should not go into voir dire with specific expectations about what you want in a juror. Instead, think about how you can frame your case for all different mindsets. Developing that kind of strategic flexibility of persuasion is the way to bring anyone to your side. Assuming the defendant is guilty."

"Wait, what?" Mary asked.

"If your defendant isn't guilty, there's an energy against a guilty verdict. It's not perfect and maybe none of your jurors will pick up on it, but if they do, it will be very hard to persuade them otherwise. As it should be. I give you Mr. Jex as an example." She raised her hand to stop Owen who was leaning forward like she was dying to interject. "Yes, he was in a car that had drugs in it, and yes, he had a prior, but he had absolutely no idea there was marijuana in the back seat console. I know this beyond a shadow of a doubt and my certainty helped convince five other jurors. Truth is a powerful thing."

The conference room door rattled, and Kira walked in. The room was quiet as she entered, and Summer figured Mary and Owen were busy trying to think of ways to ditch her so they could go back to working on the case their old way and not with some crazy mind reader pushing her theories on mind-bending juries. Kira glanced her way and Summer caught the hint of animosity, but she met it with a big smile. "Hi, Kira, nice to see you again."

Kira mumbled something that sounded a little like "hello" and focused her attention on Owen. "He's here. Are you ready for him?"

"Give us a minute." Owen held up her phone. "I'll text you as soon as we're ready."

Kira frowned. "Yeah, okay. You're the boss." She stepped out of the room and let the door slam against the frame.

Owen sighed and Mary said, "Don't mind her. She's cranky, but it's not about you."

Summer was pretty sure that wasn't true. She was certain Kira had a thing for Owen, so anyone who was lucky enough to have Owen's focus would draw Kira's ire. The question was, did Owen have a thing for Kira? She listened to the quiet for a few moments but didn't pick up on anything to tip her off. Whatever Owen's feelings were about Kira, they were guarded, which might mean she didn't want to expose their relationship if there was one. Whatever. It wasn't any of her business, but damn if she didn't really, really want to know.

"Before we bring this witness in," Owen said. "Tell me everything you already know about him. And not just what you told the duty sergeant when you called the precinct. I want to know everything."

"What I knew then or now?"

"Both."

Summer got it. This was a test, but Owen didn't have an objective way to measure her truth-telling, so she was trying to box her in on what she already knew about Leo Joule in case she tripped up. "Before I called, I only knew a few things. I ran into him at the courthouse the day I was here for Mr. Jex's trial. He asked me where to find one of the courtrooms, and I suggested he talk to the security guards. I got a strong feeling of danger from him—not that he was dangerous, but that danger surrounded him." She shook her head, anticipating Owen's question. "It wasn't any more specific than that."

She closed her eyes and relived the experience, her senses flooding with anxiety and an urgent impulse to flee. Accompanied by the strong desire for Thai food. "Wait. I remember immediately craving Thai food, and the name of this place I'd never been popped in my head. Simply Thai. Nan and Faith and I went there for dinner. I had another experience near the restaurant, closer to one of those pay lots downtown."

"What kind of experience?" Mary asked.

"It's hard to explain because the details are vague, but someone grabbed me from behind and choked me. I didn't see who and they didn't say anything else, but it wasn't me they were choking. Someone was showing me what was happening."

Owen furrowed her brow. "What do you mean by that?"

"It's hard to explain, but while I felt like I was being choked in the moment, I could see the action from two vantage points. Me, being choked and also me, standing off to the side watching me being choked."

"That sounds like one of those out-of-body, near-death experiences," Mary said. "Where people report they are floating above their body and can see what's happening but can't do anything to change it until they get back inside."

"It's a lot like that. The difference was I know it wasn't happening to me because the victim's voice wasn't mine. I felt all the sensations but still experienced nothing specific enough to alert the police. Then I started having dreams where I still felt like I was choking, but the other me, the one standing off to the side was able to register more details. I recognized the place, the tiny scar on the victim's face. I talked about it with Nan and we decided I should call it in even if I sounded like a wacko." She smiled, hoping to add some levity to the room. "The next morning, Owen and Kira showed up on my doorstep. And here we are."

"And where is that, exactly?" Kira asked. "Have your special powers led you to any special insights about the case?"

Summer spotted Owen glaring at Kira, and she spoke quickly to keep Owen from fighting her battles. "I don't have any special powers. I just reported what I saw. The way I saw it might be unconventional, but I'm no different than anyone who comes forward with information about a crime."

"How about we bring in Joule and talk to him?" Mary said.

"Great idea," Owen replied. "And, Summer?"

"Yes?"

"I'd like you to take the lead on this. Walk him through what he remembers about the night of the murder. Mary and I will ask any follow-up questions after you're done. Okay?"

Summer tensed for a moment, knowing what a huge step it was for Owen to hand over the reins in this way, and appreciating the gesture of confidence. She sensed Owen wouldn't appreciate her making a big deal of it, though, so she kept her response simple even though she wanted to be much more effusive. "Okay."

Maybe she'd have a chance later to show Owen her appreciation. In private.

Chapter Thirteen

Owen watched while Summer lobbed gentle questions at Joule. Observing Summer in action, Owen reflected she would make a great attorney, able to get witnesses to open up and be at ease. They hadn't learned anything new about the case from this meeting, but she knew Joule would be ready to face anything the defense attorney might throw his way during trial after Summer's deft handling.

When they were done talking to Joule, Owen asked him to wait outside.

"I'll run him home," Kira said, glancing at her phone. "It's six now. Are we meeting back here later?"

"I'm going to have to bail," Mary said, patting her stomach. "I haven't seen Jack all week and I promised him I'd make an extended appearance tonight so he can check the baby bump and I can get a good night's sleep. Doctor's orders. I'll work on prep for the pretrial motions that are still pending, but I can do that from home."

Owen considered her options and quickly settled on the only one that appealed to her—spending time with Summer. Alone. "That settles it. I'm going to work on my opening. Kira, if you have all the information you need to get the rest of the witness subpoenas served, then there's no need for you to come in this weekend. Oh, but try the mayor's office again. I'd like at least a few minutes with him before he testifies, but it can be the day of. If anything else comes up, we'll call you."

"Yeah, sure. You know me. Always available when you need something at the last minute and there's no one else to help out." Kira left the room in a huff, letting the door slam against the frame again in a way that could plausibly be called an accident, but which Owen knew was a clear message Kira was angry and tired of acting like things were fine between them.

Mary jerked her chin toward the door. "You're going to take care of that, right?"

"Yes. Definitely," Owen said, wanting to shut down the conversation before Mary got into more detail. She didn't want to have this conversation at all and definitely not in front of Summer. She watched Mary gather her things. "You want me to help you carry some of that?"

"And ruin my practice for carrying around a toddler? Not even." She tucked a large folder under her arm and balanced another against her chest. "Summer, it was nice to see you again. Have a good weekend. O, stay out of trouble. I'll talk to you on Sunday."

Owen watched her clear the door while she tried to think of a way to keep Summer from leaving too.

"You didn't have to send Kira away on my account," Summer said. "I saw the way you reacted when she was coming after me. I can handle myself with Kira. I've dealt with plenty of people like her over the years."

"She overstepped."

"She asked hard questions. With an attitude, yes, but there's nothing wrong with asking questions when you're skeptical."

"True, but this was about more than that."

"I know. It's fairly obvious she has a thing for you," Summer said.

"There's nothing going on between us. Not anymore." Owen immediately had mixed feelings about the overshare.

"Some people take longer to get past things than others." Summer pointed at the door. "She may take a while, but she'll get there eventually." She bit her bottom lip like she was considering what to say next, and Owen found the move adorable. "If you want to keep working or…whatever, I can stay."

Could "whatever" be more suggestive? Owen's body flushed with warmth as her mind wandered to many different kinds of "whatever," all involving Summer Byrne.

"I do want you to stick around, but I need to get out of here. I need a night away from the whiteboard and the witness files. Besides, I'm hungry and the cafeteria's closed and I'm kind of over French fries for now. Your home-cooked food has spoiled my junk food self."

Summer beamed. "I'm sure I could whip something up for you."

"I would love that, but I was thinking maybe we could do something different. I can't cook, but I do have some of the best restaurants in Dallas on speed dial. If you don't think it's weird, we could go to my place and order in."

She waited with trepidation for Summer's response, praying she hadn't overstepped. What had she been thinking, inviting Summer into her home? Her intentions were a mixed bag. Yes, she had a large, well-appointed kitchen worthy of any gourmet, but she had no intention of cooking. And yes, she had a streamlined office setup at home that was much more efficient and comfortable than her county office, but her mind was no longer focused on work. All she wanted, all she could think about, was getting a few hours alone with Summer, but what exactly those few hours would consist of was completely up in the air. Was she being inappropriate here? Was her attraction to Summer causing her to make poor choices? "Or we could go out to eat if you'd rather not come to my place." She waved a hand in an effort to signal it didn't matter either way.

Summer caught her hand mid-wave. "I'd love to have dinner with you. And I'd rather stay in than go out if that's okay."

Owen looked at their clasped hands for a second before reluctantly letting go. "It's perfect."

Twenty minutes later, Owen pulled into the circle drive in front of her building and checked her rearview mirror where she saw Summer in the car directly behind her. She handed her keys to the valet and slipped him some cash and pointed at Summer's vehicle. "Vincent, she's my guest. Take good care of her, will you?"

Vincent tipped his hat. "You got it, Ms. Lassiter."

Owen stepped under the large awning and waited for Summer to join her.

"You have to warn a girl when there's going to be a valet," Summer said, "I don't have any cash on me."

"Already handled." Owen pointed to the door. "Ready?"

"Very."

The one word was full of portent. Owen nodded at the doorman and motioned for Summer to go first, placing her hand on Summer's back as she followed her into the building. Summer leaned into her light touch, and it felt perfectly natural to ease her hand around and encircle Summer's waist as they walked through the lobby to the elevator. Inside the elevator, Owen inserted a keycard, punched the button for the top floor, and braced for a reaction. The first time she'd brought Kira home with her, she'd spent the entire ride to the penthouse musing how much it cost to live in a place like this, and she'd heard the accusation mixed with curiosity about how she could afford to live here on her county salary.

"I bet you have an amazing view," Summer said, her face beaming.

The simple observation was genuine and earnest and sounded nothing at all like Kira's attempt to dig past her privacy. Owen let down her guard and returned the smile. "I do." Now that she'd owned it, she decided to go all in and her voice cracked as she spoke. "I can't wait to show it to you."

Owen's hand shook slightly as she led the way from the elevator into her apartment. Aside from Kira and a few other women she barely remembered, she rarely had guests and never ones who made her heart beat as fast as Summer did. The motion-activated lights turned on as they entered, and she watched Summer as she took in the room.

"What a beautiful space," Summer said, walking farther into the room. "I love the decor. It's very you."

"That sounds like a compliment, but I'm not entirely sure."

Summer stepped closer to her and grasped her lapel. "Sharp, tailored, tasteful. Perfect."

"I'm far from perfect," Owen whispered.

Summer leaned closer. "That's for me to say. Eye of the beholder and all."

They were inches apart, and Owen's breath went shallow as she stared into Summer's eyes, barely able to remember what they'd been talking about. Her gaze dropped to Summer's lips, full and kissable, and she was consumed with wondering how they would taste. The heat between them was undeniable, a force she couldn't and didn't want to resist. But she should. Shouldn't she? "Summer…" It was all she could manage to say. Would it be enough to break the spell?

"Owen."

"Yes?"

"If you don't kiss me soon, I'm going to lose my mind."

Owen reached up and placed a hand on either side of Summer's face and leaned down, letting her lips graze Summer's. After a few gentle presses, she ran her tongue along Summer's lips, nudging them open and she eased her way inside, melting in the heat of their touch. Summer ran her hands along the inside of her jacket and tugged her shirt from her waistband and began stroking her skin. Owen wanted to burst out of her clothes like the Hulk, transforming into the person Summer wanted her to be, the person *she* wanted to be. Open to sharing her feelings, her hopes, her dreams with another person, and overcoming the fear that came with being vulnerable.

The idea of it was overwhelming, and Owen stepped back, still in Summer's embrace, but their connection was now more tenuous.

"Are you okay?" Summer asked, her gaze intent and infused with caring.

"I don't know." Owen straightened her jacket, needing the protection her armor afforded her. "I'm sorry. I know we're supposed to be working. I shouldn't have kissed you like that." She grimaced. "Or at all, really."

Summer kept her hands in place under Owen's jacket and she didn't move. "Are you really sorry?" She stepped closer. "Because I'm not. I'm glad to be here. With you." She licked her lips. "And that kiss? It was smoking hot and I want to do it again." She eased her hands from Owen's side. "When you're ready."

She was ready. She was barely able to continue standing ready, but practicality told her to wait. She could almost hear Mary's voice, telling her not to get involved with someone at work, but she didn't care. Every nerve ending in her body was telling her not to care. Summer wasn't just someone she worked with. Their attraction was an undeniable force. She could try to ignore the overwhelming urge to take Summer to bed. They could order food and eat and work and pretend the connection between them didn't exist, but Owen knew she'd be worthless without exploring these feelings, without satisfying the ache between her legs, the ache that thrummed through her entire body.

"I'm ready now." She let out a pent-up breath. "Right now."

Summer pulled her close and whispered in her ear, the heat of Summer's breath taking her desire to new heights.

"Take me to your bedroom, please."

❖

From the moment Owen had shown up on Nan's doorstep a couple of weeks ago, she'd been full of surprises, but Summer had been completely unprepared for Owen to invite her into what she could tell was her most private of places. Every element of energy in this gorgeous apartment screamed Owen. Expensive, impeccably appointed—all the trappings of someone who had almost everything. Guarded and quiet, the atmosphere simmered with loneliness brewing below the surface.

And then Owen kissed her. Hot, hard, wet kisses. Lush and lingering, eager and insistent. The kind of kisses that shatter resistance. Not that she'd come here ready to resist. She reached for Owen's hand and followed her down the hall, excited and ready for whatever happened next.

Owen stopped at an open door and turned and stood in the threshold. Her eyes were dark and smoldering and when she ducked her head and caught Summer's lips in her own, Summer's knees buckled against the weight of her arousal.

"Are you okay?" Owen asked, wrapping Summer in her arms and holding her close.

Summer smiled. "Okay is not the word I would use. Excited, aroused." She slid her hands under Owen's jacket again and eased them up into the sleeves. "I love your clothes. They are perfectly tailored, and you look amazing in them." She pushed up over Owen's shoulders, and the jacket dropped to the floor. "But I think I'm going to love touching your naked skin more."

She didn't wait for a reply before beginning to unbutton Owen's crisp white shirt. Owen kissed her neck as she fiddled with the buttons. It was hard to keep up with what she was doing when Owen was setting her body on fire with alternating light and hard touches from her lips and her tongue. She couldn't remember the last time she'd felt this way—desired, aroused, utterly on fire—and she wanted to speed up and slow down all at once. The last button gave her fits until Owen's hands closed over hers and deftly slipped it free. Summer leaned back and sucked in a breath while Owen shed her shirt and bra. She was heart-stompingly gorgeous. "Wow."

Owen's smile was tentative. "Is that a good wow?"

Summer wiped a hand across her forehead. "It's a 'hey, it's getting hot in here' wow." She stepped closer and traced Owen's naked breasts with her fingers. "You. Are. Beautiful." She pointed to the king-sized bed across the room with its perfectly made up spread. "Is that bed just for show or can we use it?"

"Oh, we can use it." Owen arched into her touch and moaned. "Please, let's use it."

Summer dropped her other hand to the zipper on Owen's pants and tugged it open. She slipped her hand in, and while she continued the breast play, she gently ran a finger along the fabric covering Owen's sex. Owen thrust against her finger and Summer followed the encouragement by easing her finger underneath the cloth, her moans joining Owen's as she touched the slick folds of Owen's sex. "You're so wet."

"I want you." Owen pulled at her blouse. "I want to feel your skin against mine. Please."

Summer stilled her fingers and led them toward the bed. She motioned for Owen to sit on the edge and she pulled off her pants and underwear before easing her back against the pillows. While Owen watched, she slowly undressed, trepidatiously at first, but with growing confidence as Owen signaled her pleasure by urging her to hurry. When she was completely naked, she crawled into the bed and eased her body along the length of Owen's, enjoying the delicious delight of setting off sparks between them. She kissed Owen again, a deeper kiss this time, a signal of the way she wanted to touch the rest of her body, slowly, deeply, with ever increasing passion.

"You are the best kisser ever," Owen said, her breath ragged.

"It's been a while. I was worried I'd be rusty, but I think you inspire the best in me."

Owen ran her fingers through Summer's hair. "If this is rusty, you should always be rusty. Never not be rusty." She smiled, a slow, hot, delicious smile.

Summer nipped her lips in a move designed to tease and Owen moaned again. She was loving having this kind of power, to pleasure Owen, to draw her out of her buttoned-up shell. "I love how expressive you are. It inspires me."

"Is that so? What are you inspired to do right now?"

Summer answered by inching lower and circling her tongue around Owen's nipple, enjoying the way it hardened in her mouth. She tugged and teased it to a fine point, and then closed her mouth over it completely, losing herself to the sensation of experiencing Owen in such an intimate way. She nipped and teased and lavished Owen with her tongue and then moved to her other breast and repeated each move, determined to keep it slow, but straining against the desire to bring Owen to orgasm right now.

She was lost in the feel of her when she felt a long, slow stroke through the wetness between her own legs. Once, twice, a long pause, then there it was again, and her body bucked against Owen's hand. She propped up on her elbows and rolled to her side, keeping her hand on Owen's chest and her eyes on Owen's, pleased to find them dark and hazy with desire. While Owen watched her, she reached down and stroked her way down Owen's abdomen, trailing her fingers along the tense muscles and eagerly anticipating the moment they would be able to relax when Owen cried out with release. Every ounce of her being was focused on Owen's pleasure, and Owen touching her only intensified her mission. She dipped a finger in Owen's sex and groaned when Owen ground against her hand. "You feel incredible. So wet."

"Yes." Owen breathed deep. "Ready."

Summer slid another finger in, only slightly, before easing back out and in again while she traced circles around Owen's clit with her thumb. "So ready." She kept her hand in place and eased her way down along Owen's side, missing her touch but so excited about what would happen next she embraced the sacrifice. Back between Owen's legs, she dipped her fingers lower and replaced them with her tongue, slowly teasing her way to Owen's wet, hot center.

"Oh my God, you are amazing."

Taking her confidence from Owen's cries, Summer flattened her tongue and increased the speed and pressure of each pass, taking Owen to the brink and then backing away.

Owen's body came off the bed and into her mouth, arching, grinding, seeking release, and finally Summer could deny her no more. She entered Owen with her fingers and brought her to orgasm with strong strokes of her tongue, reveling in her cries of pleasure and ecstatic to be able to give her this release.

When Owen lay spent in her arms, she held her tight. She didn't need to read Owen's mind to know she was sated. They'd been in perfect sync since they'd fallen into bed, and Summer marveled at the strength of their connection. "You were incredible."

Owen looked up from where she lay on her shoulder and kissed her cheek. "Um, you. You were the incredible one. I'm just the lucky person who got to experience the most amazing sex I've ever had."

"The 'most amazing'?" Summer raised an eyebrow. "That's a pretty big statement."

"And totally true." Owen drew her finger down Summer's chest and traced the nipple closer to her. "I can only think of one thing that could be better."

Summer's breath caught as Owen's touch grew more intense. "Tell me."

Owen rolled onto her side and dipped her head toward Summer's breast. "How about I show you?"

Thinking there could be no better way to communicate, Summer arched into Owen's mouth and surrendered to her touch.

❖

Owen woke to a dark room with Summer tucked in the crook of her arm and a sense of peace she hadn't felt in a very long time. Besides Kira, only a few other women had been here, in her sanctuary, but their encounters had been carefully choreographed and she'd remained in complete control for the duration, never inviting them to linger and never inviting them to more intimate acts like the cuddling that was taking place right now. Now that she'd experienced this closeness, this level of affection, how could she go back to impersonal encounters?

But impersonal encounters were low risk. Much lower risk than intimacy with someone like Summer who could somehow see inside her soul. Was her gift real? What other explanation could there be for her prescient warning about the attack on Joule? Or how she knew a simple chili dinner would be the perfect touch? She shook her head. There had to be another explanation, but right now she didn't care about anything other than the pleasure of having Summer in her bed.

She stroked Summer's blond tresses, causing her to stir and move even closer, the friction of skin against skin awakening the slow burn of arousal that was still smoldering from her last orgasm. Another difference between Summer and everyone else—she'd lost count of how many times they both had come, the destination taking a back seat to the journey. Before, all she'd cared about was release, hers and theirs, and, once achieved, she was done and ready for them to go. Looking back, she'd been selfish where her sexual partners were concerned, but she'd also denied herself the pleasure of total immersion in all the sensations of making love to a beautiful woman, a woman who knew how to give and receive pleasure with complete abandon.

Summer stirred at her side and looked up into her eyes. She was breathtaking, but for a moment Owen wished she were still asleep for fear the spell might break.

"What are you thinking?" Summer asked, her voice muddled with sleep.

"I'm guessing that's not a question you have to ask very much." Owen smiled. "Seriously, don't you want to take a stab at guessing?"

Summer propped up on her elbow. "You know what's funny?"

"That is a very open-ended question. Care to narrow it down?"

"Not once tonight have I accidentally read your mind."

"That's comforting. Are you usually reading my mind, accidentally or otherwise?"

"I would never do it on purpose, but occasionally, when I'm trying hard to figure out what someone really wants or needs, I tune in and get a strong signal. Not like they are telling me on purpose, but it's there, in the air, like a message they would say out loud if only something wasn't blocking their words."

Owen fluffed the pillow behind her head and scooted into an upright position, motioning for Summer to curl back into her arms. "Tell me more."

"That's the thing. There's nothing to tell. No voices in my head, no blocked messages trying to escape. But…"

Owen waited a few beats, but when Summer didn't say anything, she prompted her "But?"

Summer traced a finger up her chest and along her neckline, and then looked up into her eyes. "But it felt like we were in perfect sync. That has never happened to me. Never."

"Me either." Owen held her gaze for a few more moments, not wanting to break the connection. "I'm not big on letting people in."

"Tell me something I don't know," Summer said with an exaggerated roll of her eyes.

She waved a hand. "This place is my sanctuary. I won't say no one else has ever been in my bed, but not to stay, never to sleep, cuddle, whatever." The admission felt silly, and she looked away, wishing she could reel it back in.

"Hey, don't shut me out now."

Owen turned slowly and saw Summer's eyes were brimming with compassion. "Your sanctuary is beautiful. It suits you."

"It's opulent, but it's a reminder of...family. It's comforting."

"Do you want to tell me about it?"

Did she? If nothing else, she appreciated Summer asking instead of trying to intuit what she was thinking. If Summer wanted to know her background, it was a simple matter of connecting a few Google searches to get there. She didn't share her personal life with most people because she didn't want them to view her differently, but right now, in this moment, she wanted Summer to know everything about her, and she trusted the knowledge wouldn't sway Summer's opinion either way.

"My parents were killed when I was fourteen." She blurted out the words and paused. Summer grasped her hand and held tight, giving her the strength to press on. "They were mugged, walking to their car after their anniversary dinner at Dakota's downtown. It was where they celebrated every year. Dad wasn't a fan of the valet stand. His car was a custom Corvette and he figured the valets were probably joyriding the whole time he and Mom had dinner, so he insisted on parking it himself. Downtown Dallas isn't as busy at night as other cities. Not a lot of foot traffic, and they were alone on a dimly lit street when a guy pulled a gun and asked for his wallet. According to my mother, Dad forked it over."

She drummed her fingers on the bed. "The money meant nothing to him. They were rich. Crazy rich. He inherited a small fortune from my grandparents and put it toward an oil stake that struck big before I was born. I grew up in a mansion, with servants, and a garage that housed my dad's car collection. I went to the best private schools and never knew what it was to want for anything until the day they died." Summer was staring intently, and Owen felt the compassion roll off her in waves. It spurred her to keep talking.

"The guy wasn't satisfied with the wallet. He wanted my mother's wedding ring. It wasn't expensive—it was a simple gold band, but it had been my grandmother's and her mother's before that. Passed down through generations. Dad offered the guy anything he wanted. His car, large sums of money, anything, and when he refused, Dad tried to fight him off. The guy shot him in the chest and then turned and shot my mother. Dad bled out in her arms while she waited for an ambulance. She died alone at the hospital."

"How did you find out?"

"When the police showed up at our door. I was home, watching TV and sulking because my best friend, who I had a not so secret crush on, was hanging out with her boyfriend that night. The day after the funeral, the family assets were placed in a trust and I was shipped off to live with my aunt in San Antonio, who I'd met exactly once before, until I graduated from high school."

Summer grasped her hand and squeezed. "I can't even imagine how devastating it must have been for you to lose both your parents at once and then to be completely uprooted from your school, your friends."

Owen looked down at their clasped hands and found strength from Summer's comfort. "Looking back, the transition was probably the best thing that could've happened to me at that point in my life. I learned that not everyone had the same opportunities I had had, and at the end of the day, the person you should learn to count on the most is yourself."

"That's why you became a prosecutor."

"Yes. Pretty on the nose, right?"

"Only if people know your backstory, which I'm guessing you keep pretty private."

"I've only told a few people. Everyone treats me differently when they find out. I don't know if it's the money…" She paused. "It's probably the money."

"Or the fact the tragedy made you not want to get close to people for fear of losing them."

Owen smiled. "Look who's back to reading minds."

"Not even. That was Psychology 101 at its finest."

"Is that so? Then perhaps you can tell me what it means that I shared all this with you."

Summer reached up and kissed her lightly. "I'd like to think it means you trust me. And that this," she gestured at their entwined and naked bodies, "meant as much to you as it did to me."

"It was incredible," Owen replied, slightly side-stepping the question. The intimacy they'd shared meant more than she was willing to say out loud just yet, but she craved more. She reached for Summer's hand and brought it to her lips, slowly kissing her fingertips, one by one, her heart pounding as arousal pounded through her once again. "Can you stay a bit longer?"

Summer wrapped a leg between hers. "I want to, very much. I need to be home before Faith wakes up. Do you think it's dawn yet?"

Owen reached for her phone on the nightstand and checked the time. "Two a.m. You know, I never fed you dinner. Are you hungry?"

"Starving." Summer pressed her thigh between Owen's

legs. "But food is overrated. Maybe you could find another way to satisfy my hunger?"

Owen slid her hand between Summer's legs and took Summer's lips between her own, murmuring softly against them. "I'll spend the rest of the night trying."

CHAPTER FOURTEEN

Y ou spilled coffee on your shirt."

Summer looked down at the spot Nan was pointing to and sighed. She'd already changed one blouse because of a missing button, and she hoped she had another one in the closet that matched this suit. It was definitely a Monday morning. "Okay, I'll be right back." She pointed at the counter. "That's Faith's lunch. Do you mind shoving it in a bag for me?" She started toward the stairs, but Nan pulled her into a hug as she walked by.

"Take a deep breath and slow down. You're nervous, but everything is going to be fine."

Summer breathed in and out several times in slow succession. "Thanks, that helped."

"But you're still nervous."

"Yes. It's been a while."

"Since you were in court or since you were serious about someone?"

Summer's first instinct was to protest, but she knew it was pointless to pretend with Nan. She'd tiptoed in before sunrise on Saturday morning, but Nan didn't need to be awake to be aware. She was surprised Nan had waited this long to broach the topic. "Both."

"You want to talk about it?"

"Maybe, but not now. I've got to run. But I would really appreciate it if you could give Faith a ride to school."

"Done. Now go change your shirt and help Owen win her case. Bring her home for dinner when you're done."

Summer took the stairs two at a time, shaking her head at how easily Nan had reached the conclusion that she and Owen were an item after one night together. She'd talked to Owen several times since Saturday, but she hadn't seen her, and the distance was disconcerting. Owen said she needed the time alone to focus on her voir dire and opening statement, but Summer couldn't help but wonder if she was having regrets. She supposed she would find out today when she showed up for her role as jury consultant. If she could find another shirt, that was.

She rummaged through her closet and found one blouse that would work, though the sleeves were shorter than she liked. She shoved it on and was fastening the buttons when Faith burst in her room looking like a mini lawyer in the black suit she had bought her for Charlie's memorial service. "Looking sharp. What's the occasion?"

"I'm coming with you."

"Excuse me?"

"To court. It'll be educational. Besides, I don't really have a good idea about what you do, and we were just assigned a paper in English to write about what our parents do for a living. See, it'll be like homework."

Summer silently cursed the teacher who'd given such a thoughtless assignment and imagined what everyone would think if she showed up with her daughter in tow. She'd have mixed feelings about having Faith along, but the fact that this was a murder case with some gruesome testimony about Mrs.

Adams's death made her decision easy. "Aw, honey, some other time. I promise."

"You say that, but it's just to put me off. Come on, why can't I skip school for one day and come with you?"

Summer stared into the pleading face of her daughter and tried to conjure up an excuse that wasn't a typical adult "because I said so." "There won't be any space in the courtroom for you to sit, and even if there was, you'd be bored out of your mind because nothing of consequence is happening today."

"Where are you going to sit?"

"I'll be sitting with Owen at the prosecutor's table."

"And there are absolutely no other seats in the room?"

Summer worked hard to keep her tone even, but her patience was wearing thin. "Seriously, Faith. I know you have a math test today and I know it's your least favorite topic. The internet leaves no mysteries like it did back when I was in school. I got an email from Mrs. Halsworth saying you're having trouble in math. You've never had trouble in math before."

"And you've never been such a stickler for keeping tabs on me, so I guess we're even."

Nan appeared at the door. "What's all the commotion, people?"

"Mom's being unreasonable."

Summer resisted the urge to say, "Am not." She pointed toward the door. "Nan's taking you to school this morning. Don't keep her waiting."

Faith crossed her arms and sat down. "I don't feel so good."

Summer placed a hand on her forehead. "You feel fine to me. Besides, if you're too sick to go to school, you sure aren't well enough to come to the courthouse with me."

"Fine, I'll go to school. Will you at least tell Owen I said hi or is she just your friend now?"

And bam, now she knew what was wrong. Faith had asked her twice if they could invite Owen over during the rest of the weekend. She'd begged off with the excuse that Owen was deep in trial prep. Which was true, but not a complete barrier because she was fairly certain she could've talked Owen into coming over. But she hadn't. Not because she didn't want to see Owen. She did. Desperately. But she was worried she'd spend all of dinner looking at her with goo-goo eyes and telegraph that they were more than colleagues now. More than friends. She didn't want Faith, or Nan for that matter, to know more until she figured out for herself what it meant.

She knew what she wanted it to mean. She'd been falling for Owen since the day she'd walked into the courtroom looking all in charge and gorgeous, but she sensed that Owen's feelings were a jumbled mix and she didn't want to try to untangle them without her permission. Owen may have invited her into her bedroom, but she could tell Owen wasn't ready to accept her gift, and she wasn't sure she wanted to risk giving her heart to someone who couldn't embrace her completely, vibes and all. Of course, after Friday night, it might be too late to pull back now.

She pulled Faith into a hug. "I love you, kiddo, and I'm pretty sure there's plenty of Owen to go around. Go to school and take your math test. I'll bring tacos home for dinner, and I'll see if Owen has some time to get together as soon as this trial is over. Deal?"

Faith gave an exaggerated sigh. "Deal."

Summer kissed the top of her head and then dashed to her car. If she hurried she could still get to the courthouse in time to meet with Owen and Mary while the potential jurors were filling out their questionnaires.

Monday morning at the courthouse was vastly different from when she'd reported on a Friday for jury duty. There was a line out the front door that ran down the steps of the building. She remembered Owen telling her about the entrance through the parking garage by the cafeteria, so she walked down there and found it slightly easier to get in. Most of the people in line appeared to be attorneys, judging by the briefcases and tote bags, so security gave them only a cursory glance and she was through a lot faster than if she'd waited upstairs. Once in the building, she took the stairs to Owen's office and knocked on the door.

"Come in."

Summer smoothed her hands over her suit and let out a pent-up breath. She was way more nervous about seeing Owen again than she cared to admit, especially since she would be seeing her with a lot of other people around on a day when Owen's mind would be distracted by a million things none of which had anything to do with her. She reached for the doorknob, but it swung away from her before she could connect.

"You're here."

Summer stared at Owen and spotted eager pleasure in the smile on her face. "You sound surprised."

Owen looked over her shoulder and then tugged her gently into the room, shutting and locking the door behind her. She placed a hand on either side of her head and took Summer's lips between her own. The rest of the world fell away for the next few seconds and Summer lost herself in the long, slow kiss.

When Owen pulled away, it took all the fortitude she possessed not to grab her shirt and pull her back in for more.

She touched her fingertips to her lips. "That's the kind of good morning I could get used to."

"I missed you this weekend."

"I figured you'd be too busy working to miss me." Summer tried to sound upbeat, but it was hard to keep a wistfulness from her voice since she'd spent most of yesterday hoping Owen would suggest they get together.

"I may have been too busy missing you to work." Owen smiled. "I did my best to work, but I missed you in my bed."

"That makes two of us."

"My grand idea about staying apart so I could focus was a complete failure, so I was thinking we could try something else."

"What do you have in mind?"

"Have dinner with me tonight. For real this time. I really want to see you outside of this place, and maybe if I do, I'll have a better chance of focusing while we're here."

"I'd love to, but I promised Faith I'd bring tacos home for dinner." She caught the disappointed look on Owen's face. "How about joining us? I know it's not the same as having dinner with just the two of us, but she'd love to see you. She was talking about you this morning."

"And you? Would you love to see me? With tacos?"

"I would love to see you with or without tacos." She ran a finger along the edge of Owen's shirt collar. "Except you're going to have to change clothes before you come over because these shirts drive me crazy."

"It's just the shirts, huh?"

"It's the sexy combo of the shirts and you in them. Irresistible."

"Duly noted."

Owen kissed her again. A light, soft kiss. Summer could think of no better way to start the workday than with kisses from Owen, and when she heard a loud knock on the door, she realized she was the one with the fractured focus, and it was totally worth it.

❖

Owen sat at counsel table and focused on tuning out the chatter in the courtroom coming from attorneys and their clients who were dealing with day-to-day court business during this break. She and her team were in the process of reviewing their notes along with the stack of juror questionaries while the jury panel waited outside the room to find out if they'd been chosen. Normally, she'd find a quieter place to sort through her notes, but with an extra person on the prosecution team, they needed more space than the cramped quarters of the DA workroom.

The last time she'd been through this process, Summer had been standing outside with the other potential jurors, but now she was sitting beside her, ready to help pick the people who would decide the most high profile case Owen had tried to date, and drawing her attention in ways that had nothing to do with any aspect of this murder trial. The past few weeks had wrought a ton of change, and while she had doubts Summer would have anything to add to the trial team other than her proven sharp intuition, she was grateful to have Summer by her side.

Dalton, the bailiff, approached. "You've got fifteen minutes."

"We'll be ready," Owen said. She turned to Mary, Kira, and Summer. "I've got concerns about one, five, eight, fifteen, and twenty-three. That's five strikes. Talk to me about who else you think we should add to the list."

Kira pointed at the chart on the table. "Twenty has a sister with a record. She didn't raise her hand when you asked about it, but I found it when I was running names."

"Maybe she didn't think it was important," Summer said. "Considering the kind of case this is."

"And you know this how?" Kira replied, not bothering to hide her disdain for Summer's opinion.

"Just a hunch."

"Owen, I guess it's up to you," Kira said. "Are you going to start trusting hunches?" She left it implied that she meant Summer's hunches in particular.

Owen wondered if Summer knew something she wasn't sharing, but decided if she did know something definitive, she would say so. "Hunches are all we have right now. What's the sister's record?"

"Couple of DWIs. She did some jail time on the second one."

"Sounds like a toss-up to me," Mary said. She held her hands like she was balancing a scale. "DWI. Murder." She shook her head. "Bothers me a little that she didn't mention it, but it's possible she didn't know. It's not like my sisters tell me everything that happens in their lives, unless they're trying to one-up me. This isn't that."

Owen turned to Summer. "Do you like her for this case?"

"She seems neutral. She won't be a leader on the jury, and she'll follow whoever has the strongest personality as long as that person isn't completely off the rails."

Owen put a star in the box on the chart with twenty's name. "Okay, let's move on. If we're left with this group, who's the stand-out for foreperson?"

Kira pointed to the box marked nine. "This guy. He's confident, manages a large consulting business, and I bet he's used to having to hear a bunch of opinions and distill them down to one decision."

Owen nodded. Kira definitely had a point. On paper the guy was excellent foreman material, but the patronizing way he answered a few of the questions bothered her. "Mary, your thoughts?"

"He's definitely leader material. Not sure I have a good handle on which side that would fall down on, though."

Owen avoided Kira's gaze. "Summer?"

"You know, you should all go with your gut."

"Sounds like you have an opinion. Come on, share it with us." Owen watched Summer hesitate and shoot a glance at Kira before she started speaking like she was reluctant to cross her but felt like she had to.

Summer cleared her throat and started talking rapidly, like she was trying to get it all out before she could change her mind. "He's a chauvinist. He's never going to give as much weight to anything you and Mary have to say with a man leading the defense team. Add to that your victim is a woman and the defendant is a man, and his views are even more problematic. He'll bully jurors like twenty and four and seven, and they'll go his way no matter how the evidence plays out. I'd strike him."

"That was super specific," Kira said. "So much for hunches."

"This one isn't a hunch," Summer said. "His thoughts are loud and clear. If you're listening." She looked at Owen. "I bet you heard them."

Had she? She'd formed the same opinion as Summer, but she attributed her conclusion about juror nine to years of training, not some kind of psychic powers. Whatever the source, she had to make a decision and she was torn between wanting to believe she could sway juror number nine and going with Summer's analysis. Remembering back to Summer's own jury service, she decided to go with her gut. She scrawled his name on the strike list. "That's six." She held the paper in the air, and Dalton came over to collect it.

"I'll be back with the final list in a few minutes," he said as he took the paper from her hand. "Judge says she's going to seat the jury today, but then she's got to finish up a sentencing from last week's trial. If you've got any pretrial motions that still need to be heard, she'll get to those right after she wraps up the other case. We'll start back first thing in the morning for opening statements, and then she wants you to have your first few witnesses ready to go right after opening."

Owen digested the information, recalibrating for the change in plans. Her opening statement was simple and straightforward, but she'd been geared up to give it today. She was used to the roller coaster of trial, where making a solid plan was asking for disruption, but with all the press attention this case had garnered, she'd prefer not to wait. She spotted Summer looking at her with an encouraging smile.

"You got this."

Had she heard Summer's thoughts, or was she still so swept up in the afterglow that she imagined Summer's gift was real and had rubbed off on her? She returned the smile and then sprang to her feet with the rest of the group when Judge Whalen walked through the door behind the bench.

"Take a seat. I understand we have a jury," she said, pulling out a pair of readers and scanning the paper Dalton handed her. "Where's Mr. Ramsey?"

Mark Ramsey appeared from the holdover, followed by his client, who was led by a sheriff's deputy, and they both took a seat at the defense counsel table. While Dalton delivered a copy of the final jury list to both sides, Owen took a moment to assess the defendant who she'd seen exactly one other time during the course of the case. Arthur Fuentes almost looked like a regular guy, dressed in a suit and tie, although he was significantly thinner than he had been at the arraignment months ago. Obviously, jail didn't agree with him. Too bad.

She felt a light touch on her arm from behind, where Summer had taken a seat in the first row of the gallery. Summer handed her a folded piece of paper, which Owen took and surreptitiously opened out of Mary's or Kira's sightline. *Can I meet him?*

Him who? She looked back at Summer, who nodded toward Fuentes. Why did she want to meet him? She shook her head. It didn't matter why. There was no way Ramsey was going to let his client meet with anyone on the prosecution team, and Owen didn't need Summer calling anything about this case into question, not on the literal eve of trial. She wrote the request off as Summer trying to be thorough, and she stuck the note in her pocket, ready to focus on the final jury list.

Their conversation about juror number twenty had turned out to be a total waste of time since the defense had used a preemptory strike on her. As the bailiff called the names of the jurors who'd made it onto the jury, she took her time looking each one over, noting their expressions, their posture, their attentiveness, careful to keep her own expression serious but not off-putting as the judge swore them in and gave them initial instructions about what would be expected of them during the course of the trial. When Whalen dismissed them until morning, Owen felt like she had a good handle on the group and would be ready to pitch her opening statement with maximum effectiveness in the morning.

As the courtroom cleared, she addressed her group. "Kira, let the mayor and the commissioner know they are first up tomorrow, right after opening. Next, we'll have the ME, Joule, and we'll finish out with Detective Garcia. Make sure everyone is here and ready to go when it's their turn. I don't want any delays between witnesses. Mary, let's meet for lunch to go over the motions you filed this morning. I have a few suggestions for argument. Summer, will you walk me to my office?"

She waited until they were in the stairwell to say anything to Summer. "Sorry to be so abrupt back there."

"You're under a lot of pressure. I didn't mean to add to it. I figure it couldn't hurt to ask."

"Why do you want to talk to him?"

"I'm not entirely sure."

"He's guilty, Summer. No one disputes it. Joule saw him leaving the house right after the shots were fired. There's not a shred of evidence to point to someone else pulling the trigger."

Summer nodded. "I get it. I do. But there are signs that there's another layer to what happened that night. Why else would I have had the vision of Joule being attacked if not to lead me to work on this case? And Mrs. Adams appeared to me in the commissioner's office. What she said didn't make sense at the time because we were focused on whether the commissioner had anything to do with her death, but what if she was telling us to dig deeper when it came to the case overall?"

Owen hesitated. She wanted the truth as much as anyone, but she wasn't convinced Summer talking to Fuentes was going to be revelatory. "If you thought talking to Fuentes would give you some insight, why didn't you ask before the trial started?"

"Would you have let me if I had?"

Owen felt tested. Summer wanted to know if she trusted her gift, and she answered as honestly as she could. "I don't know."

"I get it," Summer said. "I didn't know talking to him might be helpful until he walked into the courtroom. Maybe I just feel the need to be thorough. Close the loop. Is there harm in trying?"

Owen wished she knew the answer. "Ramsey won't agree, and I don't want to ask for fear he'll read something into it."

Summer reached for her hand. "Hey, I get it. Forget I brought it up. Treat me like you would anyone else on your team. Your word is final, and I respect that. The last thing you need is an annoying girlfriend pestering you for special favors."

Girlfriend. Girlfriend? Had Summer just used that word in reference to her? And why wasn't she running in the opposite direction at the sound of it? Owen looked down when Summer released her hand, instantly missing the warmth of her touch.

"I didn't mean that the way it sounded."

"I'm trying to figure out what other way you might have meant it," Owen said, careful to keep her tone neutral.

A loud creak sounded and they both looked down to see a door open on the floor beneath them. Mia's intern, Tad, poked his head through and looked up at her. "Owen, Ms. Rivera would like you to join her for lunch if you're available."

It wasn't a question and Owen didn't have a choice. Mia would want a full report on jury selection and she wanted it right freaking now if she sent her intern to skulk around in stairwells to find her. So much for a few moments of alone time in her office with Summer, although instead of secret kissing, they'd probably be discussing the word "girlfriend" and what it meant to both of them, a discussion Owen couldn't possibly handle when her head was focused on the trial.

"Tell Ms. Rivera I'll be right there," Owen said to Tad. She waited until she heard the door shut again before facing Summer. "I'm sorry, but I have to go."

"I know."

"We can talk later, just not, you know, right now."

"Of course," Summer said. "After the trial is over."

"Right."

"Right."

"Okay, well, I should go," Owen said, wondering why she was more agitated than relieved that Summer was being so understanding.

Summer glanced around, and then leaned in and kissed her lightly on the cheek. "For luck. Which you don't need. You got this."

Without waiting for a response, she took the stairs back down to the floor below and disappeared out the door. Owen watched her every step and thought of a dozen things she should've said, and hoped it wasn't too late when she was finally ready to say them.

CHAPTER FIFTEEN

Summer reread the same paragraph of the police report for the sixth time before tossing it onto the coffee table and leaning back into the pillows on the couch. She'd been home for a few hours and had accomplished nothing, unable to focus on anything related to the case and unwilling to turn her attention away from it. A nagging sensation something was off had started from the moment Fuentes entered the courtroom, but she couldn't zero in on it, and trying only seemed to make her more frustrated.

"Dig deeper."

It was the same voice, the same words, she'd heard when she and Owen had met with Commissioner Adams. She'd assumed the voice was Carrie Adams signaling there was more to her death than met the eye, but what? From the moment she'd become involved with the case, every signal she'd received told her that Fuentes killed Carrie Adams. She'd picked up on Owen's suspicion that Commissioner Adams might have been involved, but would his wife be forgiving enough to plead with her to help him find his way? Nothing about her tone indicated she wanted revenge or retribution.

She closed her eyes, willing Carrie to come back and offer a better explanation for her vague pleas, but before she could settle into mediation, the front door swung open and Faith came barreling in.

"Mom, you're home. I thought you were going to be in court all day. Are we still having tacos? I'm pretty sure I aced my math test, by the way."

Summer laughed. "Who are you?" She pretended to frown. "Seriously, this morning there was this girl who looked exactly like you, but she was kind of grouchy and bullheaded. You seem like a much more pleasant version."

Faith rolled her eyes. "You're hilarious." She tossed her backpack onto the coffee table. "Hey, is that stuff for your trial?"

Summer reached for the police report before Faith could get to it. "Yes, and I shouldn't have brought it home because I'm not supposed to share it with anyone." She folded it in half and tucked it under her leg.

"Speaking of home, why are you here so early?"

Nan appeared in the door. "Yeah, why are you here so early?"

Summer tucked her feet up under her and motioned for them to sit. "I'm trying not to be offended that you both wish I wasn't home."

"Oh, we're glad you're here," Nan said, "But we both hoped you would be bringing tacos for dinner."

Tacos. Right. She'd promised Faith tacos, and she'd almost forgotten, or rather she'd pushed it from her mind because there was also supposed to be Owen joining them for tacos, and she suspected that wasn't happening after she'd gone and been a mush ball at the courthouse this morning. The idea of putting regular clothes back on and trekking back out into the world was overwhelming, and she considered telling Faith she'd make something else for dinner and they'd get tacos another time.

"Did I mention I think I aced my math test?" Faith said in a semi-disturbing display of mind-reading.

"Tacos it is. I'll go change. Want to ride with?"

"What about homework?"

"This one time you can do it after dinner." Summer figured if she could lounge around all afternoon, then she could cut Faith a little slack.

Faith fist pumped the air. "Yes."

In her room, Summer pulled on a pair of jeans and her favorite RBG T-shirt. She'd hung her suit back up from this morning, thinking she could pair it with a different blouse later in the week, assuming she wouldn't get a call from Owen saying they no longer needed her. She hoped that wouldn't happen. Why had she had to use the word "girlfriend"? It was so loaded. And so soon. Even if it didn't feel that way to her, she'd put Owen on the spot. Honestly, how did she expect Owen to react?

Faith was waiting at the front door. "Nan gave me her order."

"Cool." Summer jangled her keys. "Let's go." She felt a buzzing in her pocket. "Oh wait. Hang on." She pulled out her phone and checked the screen. Owen. "Sorry, I need to take this."

Faith sighed dramatically. "Fine. I'll wait outside."

Summer shooed her off and ducked into the den to take the call. "Hey there."

"Hey, yourself."

"I wasn't expecting to hear from you. Are you still working?"

"Kind of. I was thinking of taking a break to get something to eat."

Summer's instinct was to invite Owen over, keep their original plan, but after Owen's reaction to the girlfriend comment, she decided to tread carefully. "We were about to do the very same thing."

"Tacos?"

"You know it."

"I love tacos. All kinds. Traditional, foodie, you name it."

Summer wasn't sure what to say. It kind of sounded like Owen was angling for an invitation, but did she want to put herself out there again?

A loud cry pulled her out of her thoughts. She held the phone away from her ear to try to figure out where the sound was coming from and she heard the cry again, but it sounded more like a squeal of joy, followed by "Owen!" Definitely coming from the phone. She put it back to her ear. "What's going on? Is that Faith?"

"Hang on," Owen said.

Summer heard a muffled sound and then Faith's voice came through the line. "Owen brought tacos. Where are you?"

Summer practically ran to the front door and threw it open to find Owen and Faith standing on the front step, each holding a large bag.

Owen smiled tentatively and held out a bag. "I wasn't sure what kind you liked, so I brought a little of everything." She pointed to the bag Faith was holding. "Oh, and queso. Lots of queso."

Summer smiled back to set her at ease, although she was kind of faking it herself. "Well, get in here, taco lady." She held the door open and stepped to the side, but not before accidentally on purpose brushing against Owen to test the waters. Owen winked to show she'd clicked to her not so smooth move, and Summer took the bag from her hand and gave it to Faith.

"Take these to the kitchen, math genius. I need to talk to Owen for a minute in private."

"Okay, but don't get all caught up in 'work' stuff."

Summer watched Faith take off toward the kitchen. "Tell me she did not just use air quotes."

"Uh, I can't because she totally did."

Summer turned her attention back to Owen and all the questions that bubbled up at her sudden appearance. "Follow me," she said, leading them both into the den. She shut the door behind them, and started to speak, but Owen held up a hand to stop her.

"I overreacted. In the stairwell. You used a word I don't think anyone has used since I was in high school going to prom with some guy, but only because his best friend was dating the girl I had a crush on and I figured a double date was the closest I would ever get to her. I nearly decked him when he called me his girlfriend, and I guess I haven't figured out a civilized way to react to the word since."

Summer's brain spun as she digested Owen's words. "Wow. Okay. That was a lot."

But Owen wasn't done. "Too much really, but I wanted you to know that when *you* said the word, I liked it. More than liked it."

"If I'm hearing you correctly, what you're trying to say, but with a lot more words, is that you practically running away from me at the courthouse was not the same as you wanting to deck bad prom date guy from high school."

"Not even." Owen stepped closer. "Will you say it again? You know, so I can react appropriately."

Owen's proximity was making her warm and flustered, but should she comply? Had she said it too soon? Was she overthinking it now? Her at attention nerve endings said no and it wasn't like she had a history of jumping in too soon. No, what she felt for Owen was strong and real and completely genuine. The real question was whether Owen felt the same way. She slid her hands around Owen's waist and leaned in close to whisper in her ear, acutely conscious of how much it drove her crazy. "Do you want to be my girlfriend?"

"Oh yes. Yes, I do."

Owen punctuated her answer with a deep, slow kiss that left Summer buckling at the knees. In that moment, she forgot about tacos, the trial, and anything that didn't involve Owen's talented lips and tongue. Until the sound of the door opening jerked her back to reality.

"Are you girls planning to stay in here kissing?" Nan asked with a knowing look. "It's fine with me if you are because more tacos for me and Faith." She was gone before they could answer, shutting the door behind her.

"Did that just happen?" Owen asked.

"Oh, it did. And it's likely to happen again if you decide you want to stick around."

Owen kissed her again. A quick, light kiss this time. "Oh, I do. For as long as you'll have me." She frowned. "But what about Faith?"

"She comes with the package."

Owen laughed. "Of course she does. I mean, do I need to play it cool around her or are we coming out?"

Summer pointed at her head. "This gift? It runs in the family, so I have a feeling she already knows something is going on, hence the air quotes. Let's play it by ear and if it feels natural, we can bring it up. But in the meantime, there are tacos waiting." Summer pulled her to the door, reluctant to leave their bubble, but figuring she better get used to living outside of one if she was going to have a shot at a real relationship with Owen.

Faith and Nan had set the table and a huge tray of tacos

and several bowls of queso were waiting. Faith ushered Owen to the seat between her and Summer, and within a few minutes they were all stuffing their faces.

After her third taco, Faith tossed her napkin on the table. "I surrender. Those were amazing. Best reward for acing a math test ever." She turned to Owen. "I even got to put off homework until after dinner, but if I'd known you were coming over, I would've gotten it out of the way earlier."

"It's all good," Owen replied. "I have homework too. I have to give an opening statement in my trial tomorrow. It was supposed to be today, but it was postponed. You'd think I'd already be ready, but since I've had more time to think about it, I thought of some things I want to change."

"I wanted to go to court with Mom today, but Mom said I couldn't miss my math test. I bet it would've been a great learning experience."

"Some of the magnet schools bring high school kids to the courthouse to watch trials. Maybe you can sign up for one of those programs a couple of years from now."

"When you're my age, everything happens a couple of years from now."

Nan snorted. "Just wait until you're my age and everything happened more than a couple of years ago."

Summer watched the exchange, loving the easy interaction between her grandmother, her daughter and her—dare she say it—girlfriend. It was effortless and comfortable, and she appreciated how Owen treated Nan with deference and Faith like a very important person rather than baggage she had to accept if she wanted to get close to her. Her heart was full, and she was feeling generous, which prompted her to ask, "Owen, on a scale of G to R, what's the rating for tomorrow's opening statement?"

Owen looked surprised by the question but recovered quickly. "PG. Definitely not higher than PG."

Okay with you if I bring her along?

"Of course."

Summer was so excited Owen had not only heard her thought, but responded, she didn't notice Faith was watching them until she waved a hand in her face.

"What's going on?" Faith asked.

"How would you like to go to court with me tomorrow and listen to Owen's opening?"

Faith let out a loud whoop, gave Owen a big hug, and then descended on her with an even bigger hug and a whispered message. "I like her, Mom. Let's keep her around."

"On it, kiddo." And just like that, the bubble was broken. Summer couldn't be happier.

CHAPTER SIXTEEN

Owen read the message on her phone for the fifth time, but she still couldn't glean the underlying meaning. *Can we meet before getting started this morning? With my client.* It had come in a few minutes ago, right after she and Kira and Mary had gathered in her office to go over final details for the day ahead.

She showed it to Mary. "What do you think it means?"

"I think it means Mark Ramsey wants to meet with you before opening statements this morning."

Owen rolled her eyes. "I can tell that much on my own. You know what I'm asking."

"Maybe you should ask Summer," Kira said. "She probably knew before you got the text."

Owen resisted a smart remark, instead saying, "Have you checked downstairs to see if the mayor and the commissioner are here yet?"

"Maybe Fuentes wants a plea."

"Now? He's asking for the first time after the trial has already started?"

"Have you ever made an offer?"

"Ron floated an offer to him right after indictment, before

I took over the case. Forty years. Ramsey turned it down within an hour."

"Do you think he even took it to Fuentes?"

Owen considered for a moment. Some attorneys might reject an offer out of hand, but Ramsey was a stand-up guy. "No, he would've told him about it. That early in the case, Fuentes probably thought he should wait and see, but I would've expected an overture like this to come up before today."

"Assuming a plea is what he wants. Maybe it's something else." Mary pointed at the phone. "Only one way to find out. We have an hour before we have to be in court. You go meet with him and I'll wrangle witnesses with Kira."

"Fine. I'll try to use the jury room in the court next door. I don't want to do this in the holdover where everyone can hear. Do you mind setting it up with Dalton?"

While Mary called downstairs to secure the location, she typed a text to Ramsey and kept it short. *Meet you in fifteen minutes. Jury room for the 368th.*

They gathered their files and headed for the elevator. Owen pushed the down button and the doors immediately opened to reveal Summer and Faith standing inside. Faith was wearing a visitor badge. Owen stepped to the side to let them off.

"Are you already headed downstairs?" Summer asked. "I hope it's okay we're early."

"Hi, Owen." Faith grinned. "I was going to bring you a breakfast taco, but Mom said we didn't have time if I wanted to get a good seat. I hope it's still okay I came with."

"Bummed about the breakfast taco, but of course it's okay you're here," Owen said, doing her best to maintain a professional appearance in front of Mary, but suspecting she was failing miserably. "Mary, this is Faith, Summer's daughter.

She's doing a report on different professions and she's going to sit in for opening today."

Mary shook Faith's hand. "Nice to meet you." She pointed at the elevator. "O, I'm going to go on ahead and make sure Dalton can set up the room."

She winked before she turned and walked away, and Owen knew she'd have some explaining to do later.

"Everything okay?" Summer asked.

"Yes. Fuentes's attorney wants to meet with us before we get started, so I should get down there."

"That's okay, we'll go grab seats. I hear it's going to be a full house. You'll be great." Summer pushed the button for the elevator.

"Wait." Owen's mind whirred with a sudden impulse. "Why don't you come with me? You wanted to meet Fuentes and this is the perfect opportunity. It'll only be for a few minutes and Dalton can make sure Faith gets a good seat."

"Sure. That sounds great."

The door to the elevator opened again and they rode down to the seventh floor. In addition to the regular courthouse traffic, the hallway outside the courtroom was swimming with press, jockeying for the best position to capture images of the attorneys arriving for court. Owen avoided the crowd by ducking into the courtroom next door and leading Summer and Faith through the door by the jury box.

She pointed to the right. "We can take this hallway to Judge Whalen's courtroom next door." At that moment, Dalton stepped out of a room to their left. "Hi, Dalton. Are we all set?"

He nodded. "Mary's already in there. If it's okay with you, I'll let Kira bring Fuentes over. I've got to deal with a few things for the judge before we get started."

"Thanks for your help." She put a hand on Faith's shoulder.

"This is Faith, Summer's daughter. Would you mind taking her over with you so she can snag a seat?"

"Not in the least." Dalton reached out and took Faith's hand. "Come on. I'll show you the best place to sit to see everything."

Faith waved at them as she walked away.

"She's never going to stop talking about this," Summer said. "You've made her year."

"Until she falls asleep watching all the boring bits." She pointed at the jury room where they were going to meet with Fuentes. "Thanks for doing this. I value your impressions."

"Even if you still think they're a bit on the woo-woo side."

"I'm trying."

"I know."

They stood staring at each other for a moment, and Owen wished the trial was over and they could blow off the rest of the day doing something fun.

"Me too," Summer said. "But it'll be over soon enough."

"Hey, you did that on purpose."

"Read your mind? I couldn't help it. You were thinking really loudly."

"Or maybe you're just getting to know me." Owen didn't care which it was as long as she could spend more time with Summer, and the sooner they finished this trial, the sooner she could indulge her desires. She placed her hand on the door. "Ready?"

Summer followed Owen through the door, and noted it was set up exactly like the jury room she'd spent several hours in a few weeks ago. Large table ringed with chairs. A counter off to the side with a coffee maker and a random assortment of mugs. Mark Ramsey was sitting at the table by himself and he looked up when she and Owen entered. She followed Owen's lead and sat on the same side of the table as her, leaving the seat next to Ramsey open for his client.

"Kira will be here in a minute with Fuentes," Owen said.

"That's okay. I want to go ahead and fill you in before he gets here." Mark flipped to a sheet in his notebook. "I found out yesterday that Arthur has stage four pancreatic cancer."

Owen's eyes widened. "And you just found this out? How is that possible?"

"Because he didn't tell anyone. I found out by accident. I contacted his wife, make that ex-wife, to see if she had any records of counseling he'd received for mental health issues— for mitigation in case we get to sentencing. Arthur said he didn't keep any papers and didn't want me to bother, but I felt like I needed to dig a little deeper. She gave me a packet of medical bills, most of which had never been opened." He sighed. "I'm probably breaking all kinds of HIPAA rules telling you all of this, but it appears he was diagnosed last year and now the only treatment available is palliative. He's dying."

"I'm not sure what I'm supposed to do with this information," Owen said. "What are you asking for?"

"I'm asking you to show some mercy and offer him a deal. Something where he doesn't have to spend the rest of his life in prison."

"But you're telling me he's dying. How long does he have?"

"Not long." Summer put a hand up to her mouth as if she could shove the words back inside. "Sorry. My grandfather died of it. Once you reach stage four, the survival rate is very low."

"She's right," Mark said. "I don't have a medical answer,

if that's what you're looking for, but he's looking at probably less than a year."

"And you want me to let him plead in exchange for less than a year on a murder charge?" Owen asked.

"If you go through with the trial and get a conviction, he could get compassionate release."

"Or you could present evidence during sentencing about his medical condition. If the jury sympathizes with him, they could sentence him on the low end."

"With his priors, they still couldn't give him anything below twenty years."

"Wait a minute. Now I get it. You're asking me to reduce the charge. Take the prior convictions off the indictment and open up the range of punishment."

"I get it's a long shot," Mark said, his tone pleading. "Will you at least talk to him before you decide?"

Owen looked at Summer like she was seeking advice, and Summer was conflicted, but she didn't feel like she could decide anything in the abstract and neither could Owen. *It won't hurt to meet him.*

Owen nodded at her and turned to Mark. "No promises, but I'll listen to what he has to say."

As if on cue, Kira walked through the door with Fuentes. He was wearing the same suit as he had been the day before, but with no jury in sight, he was still cuffed at the ankles and hands. She led him to the chair next to Ramsey and stood a couple of feet behind. Summer could tell Kira was surprised to see her there, but she avoided eye contact and faux scribbled some notes in the pad she'd brought with her in an effort to avoid attracting attention.

Mark turned to his client. "Arthur, I just filled Ms. Lassiter in on your medical situation. She may have a few questions for you. Go ahead and tell her whatever she wants to know."

"NO!"

Summer's head whipped up from her notebook at the loud declarative, but everyone was sitting quietly as if nothing had happened. She met Fuentes's eyes, and immediately a loud string of phrases started playing on a loop. *"Keep your mouth shut and we'll take care of your kids." "Scare her." "She wasn't supposed to die. She fought back." "Keep your mouth shut if you want us to take care of your kids." "Scare her." "She wasn't supposed to die. She fought back." "Keep your mouth shut. Keep your mouth shut. Keep your mouth shut."*

The litany grew louder and louder. Summer put her hands to her ears, but it wouldn't abate, and the constant pounding was making her nauseous.

"Are you okay?"

Owen's voice broke the pounding cycle, and Summer felt the nausea ebb away. "Sorry, I felt a little faint." She swallowed hard. "I'm okay now."

Owen stared at her for a moment like she wanted to say something else, before turning back to Fuentes. "Your attorney tells me you're ill and you'd like to plead guilty in exchange for a light sentence." She waited a beat, but Fuentes didn't respond. "Do you have anything to say about that?"

Fuentes barely looked up before he shook his head.

"Keep your mouth shut. Keep your mouth shut."

Summer looked around, but no one else appeared to be registering the words.

"Mr. Fuentes, I can't do anything for you if you won't talk. I'm not saying a plea deal is even an option, but if it is, you're going to have to swear out a confession in open court. Are you prepared to do that?"

"Keep your mouth shut. Keep your mouth shut. Keep your mouth shut."

SPIRIT OF THE LAW

"Who is telling you not to talk? Who hired you to threaten Carrie Adams? What did they promise you in return?"

Summer could hear the questions, each one louder than the other, but it wasn't until she noticed everyone in the room staring in her direction that she realized she'd been the one asking. Holy shit. Owen was looking at her like she'd grown a second head and she wanted to run from the room, but another voice vied for her attention and compelled her to stay.

"He didn't do this on his own. I fought back and the gun went off. He didn't mean to kill me until it was too late. Dig deeper."

Carrie Adams. Summer could almost see her now, standing behind Fuentes, a shadowy figure with a vague resemblance to the photo she'd seen in the war room. Summer closed her eyes and saw the whole scene play out. Fuentes creeping up behind her. He said something she couldn't make out. Carrie turned, saw him, and immediately tried to fight him off. There was a struggle and the gun went off, both of them surprised to see the red blossom across Carrie's abdomen.

"You didn't go there to kill her, but you panicked. Why won't you tell us what happened? Who hired you?"

Fuentes sat ramrod straight, refusing to make eye contact with her, but Owen was already out of her seat, leading her to the door. When they were on the other side of it, the spell broke again and Summer sagged against the wall, dizzy and spent.

"What the hell just happened?"

Owen was standing with her hands on her hips, her eyes blazing with anger. Summer didn't blame Owen for her reaction since she'd only heard one side of the conversation, but it was her job to make her understand. She had to make her understand. "He wasn't acting on his own. Someone paid him to threaten Carrie Adams or promised to take care of his kids after he died, but when he showed up at the house, she fought him, and the gun went off. He panicked and fired twice more before he ran out of the house. The police didn't find anything taken from the house because he wasn't there for any reason other than to threaten Mrs. Adams. The question is who hired him and why?"

"Do you realize how crazy you sound right now?"

Summer looked into Owen's eyes, but gone was the ardent lover who'd stolen kisses from her in her office yesterday morning and shared tacos with her family last night. That person was replaced by someone who thought she was a crackpot. Summer took a deep breath to steady her voice and spoke with as much confidence as she could muster. "Owen, there's a bigger picture here. You can walk into that courtroom, convince a jury to convict that man, and close this case, but I'm telling you something else is going on and you are going to wish you'd dug deeper to get to the truth."

"Why did you quit your job in Santa Cruz?"

Owen's question was a gut punch, but Summer braced for the impact of this conversation. "I don't like to talk about it. Besides, it's not like you can't google it."

"I did. People were upset with the DA for relying on your 'gift' to prosecute his cases, but there was something else, wasn't there?"

"Yes." Summer took a deep breath, dreading telling Owen about her failure, but knowing she had to. "A girl died because I was wrong. I thought I had answers, but I was wrong. If you looked me up, you must know that already."

Owen nodded. "Because you didn't know where she was. How could you have? You were guessing." She clenched her jaw and her gentle resignation turned to anger. "Mia shouldn't have made me hire you." She pointed at the door. "That guy in there has been in the system before and he knows how to work it. He's working you. Those vibes you're getting? It's him playing on your sympathy and you're filling in the rest. We're done with the extrasensory consulting. This 'gift' you supposedly have is a distraction. I need you to leave, so I can focus on winning this case on the facts and the evidence, not wild conjecture."

Summer wanted to argue, but she knew Owen wasn't in a place where she would hear anything she had to say. In less than thirty minutes, the trial would start, and she was under tremendous pressure to perform, to win. Summer couldn't blame her for being angry, for not wanting to listen to anything that would disrupt her theory of the case. So, yeah, she wasn't surprised at Owen's response, but damn, she was disappointed.

❖

"What the hell happened in there?" Kira asked.

Owen was standing in the empty jury room trying to process the answer to that very question. She sure didn't need Kira breathing down her neck about it. She'd told Mark no plea deal, especially since Fuentes didn't appear inclined to say anything to anyone beyond the supposed telegraphed thoughts he'd sent to Summer, but they didn't prove Fuentes was innocent, only less culpable, assuming they were even true.

Whatever had just happened, she needed to move past it and focus on her opening statement and the first few witnesses. "Is the mayor here?"

Kira nodded. "You want me to bring him back?"

"Yes." Owen knew she was being unnecessarily curt, but she didn't have any extra energy for pleasantries, not to mention she was embarrassed that Kira had witnessed Summer's meltdown during the meeting with Fuentes. Maybe meltdown was a strong word, but Summer's behavior was like nothing she'd ever seen. She'd seemed almost possessed, like she was echoing the words of someone else, parroting questions only she could hear.

Which was exactly what a medium would do—channel messages from the dead. Right? Assuming she believed Summer really was getting messages from the dead, was Carrie Adams the one doing the talking, and was she calling into question Fuentes's culpability? Seemed unlikely considering she was dead as a direct result of his actions. But what had Summer asked Fuentes? *Who hired you?* In the moment, she'd thought the question was out of line, but hadn't she had similar thoughts with regard to Commissioner Adams? Why had she been so quick to dismiss Summer on the same topic?

"You wanted to see me?"

Mayor Heller filled the doorway with his imposing frame. Years ago, he'd played college ball and would've gone pro but for a debilitating knee injury that took him out of commission his senior year. He'd traded his sports stardom for a political career that consisted of several terms in the state legislature and back-to-back terms as mayor of Dallas. Unlike Commissioner Adams who was universally liked, Heller had a reputation as a bully, ramming his agenda down the throats of his adversaries, which made them an odd couple whenever they joined forces on an issue that affected the city.

She invited him to have a seat. "I won't keep you long. I just wanted to review your testimony one more time before I put you on the stand today."

"Happy to help."

Owen took him through a few foundational questions about how he knew Commissioner Adams, and then got into the meat of his testimony, a preemptive defense to any claim Ramsey might make that the police had been negligent in their investigation by not considering the commissioner as a suspect. "How long were you with Commissioner Adams on the evening of his wife's death?"

"We'd met for drinks around five, and after a couple of rounds, we decided to grab dinner, so we moved to a table in the restaurant. You'd have to check the tab for the exact time, but I was with him until he got the call that his house had been broken into."

Owen asked a couple more questions and decided she was satisfied they didn't need to cover anything else. "Thanks for being here this morning. I know it's hard to wait around when I'm sure you have a lot on your schedule."

"This is the most important thing on my schedule today." He shook his head. "Such a tragedy."

He said the right things, but it sounded more like a sound bite than actual sympathy for Carrie Adams or the commissioner. She stood to signal they were done, but he didn't move out of his chair.

"I heard a rumor you're thinking about a deal. Is that true?"

"Who told you that?"

"Your investigator. She also mentioned you've got some kind of psychic working on this case and the psychic thinks this guy Fuentes was hired to kill Adams's wife. You're not taking that seriously, are you? I thought he had an extensive record of breaking into houses."

While he was talking, the hair on the back of Owen's neck stood up, but she couldn't put her finger on what was causing the alarm. On top of that, she was boiling mad at Kira for blabbing about Summer to the mayor. Kira had crossed a line.

It was her own fault for thinking Kira's growing animosity would eventually dissipate, but if they weren't already knee-deep in this case, she'd kick her off the team right now. "We take all leads seriously, Mr. Mayor. I'm sure you want us to be thorough, don't you?" She started walking toward the door, and he stood, finally getting the hint she was ready for him to leave.

She waited until he was out of sight and then texted Kira, asking her to come back to the jury room. When Kira arrived, she didn't bother with any niceties. "Have you seen Adams?"

"About that. He's here but his aide said he was talking to Summer."

Dammit. Could things spiral any more out of control? Owen looked at her watch. She should already be in the courtroom and Mary was probably wondering where she was. She definitely wanted Adams in there, representing the victim, before they got started, but she also wanted to talk to Summer. "Where are they?"

"I don't know."

"What do you mean you don't know?"

"The aide said they got into the elevator and he wasn't sure where they were going. I think he was under the impression that Summer was part of the prosecution team."

Owen heard the derisive tone in Kira's voice and her immediate instinct was to defend Summer. "She *is* part of the prosecution team, which is more than I can say for you. Since when do you think it's okay to blab about conversations we have behind closed doors to witnesses in a case? Yes, the mayor told me what you said about Summer."

Kira's face flushed red. Owen felt bad for blowing up at her now when she hadn't stood up for Summer in the moment. Why hadn't that been her first instinct when Summer tried to tell her something was off about Fuentes or about the murder? Were the voices Summer heard any less credible than her own gut feelings? She needed to find Summer and make things right, and she knew one person who might know where she was.

CHAPTER SEVENTEEN

Summer led the commissioner into Owen's office. She hoped Owen would forgive her when she found out what she was up to, but that ship might've sailed.

"Are you going to take me through a trial run of my testimony?"

That's what she'd told his aide. She'd also told him that she had to do it in private and given some cooked-up explanation that was loosely grounded in the rules of evidence, but mostly made up.

"In a minute, but first I wanted to talk to you about your wife. I know this sounds crazy, but when Owen and I met with you in your office, your wife was there. Her spirit. She's been looking out for you and she thinks you're in trouble."

He crossed his arms and frowned at her. "You're right, that does sound crazy. And it's not very nice. I miss her more than you can imagine, but she's gone. I've spent every day since she died trying to get used to that fact."

I need a sign. Something to convince him you're here. It didn't always work, and it felt like old school parlor magic, but it didn't hurt to ask a spirit for some kind of bona fide to prove her credibility. Seconds passed. She wasn't getting anything, and she could tell Adams was getting impatient with her. He was shifting in his chair, and any minute now, he was going to get up and leave.

The picture appeared in her head, hazy, but clear enough. Script spelling out the words "To my Rose." She could hear a tune, faint, but she recognized it because Faith had come home from school, humming it soon after they moved to Dallas. "The Yellow Rose of Texas." None of it made any sense to her, but it was all she had. "You called her Rose. To my Rose." She started humming the tune, feeling foolish and hoping it worked.

"The music box. How did you know? I gave it to her for our first anniversary and she kept it all these years."

"You loved her very much."

He sank into a chair, looking defeated. "I did."

"She loves you too."

He looked at her with imploring eyes. "She wouldn't say that now."

"Why? She knows you're in trouble, but she doesn't blame you for it." Summer reached for his hand. "She told me so I can help you. I promise I can help you," she said, hoping it was true. "I know that Arthur Fuentes killed your wife, but I don't think it was a botched burglary. I think someone hired him to do it. Do you know who could have done that?"

"Did you know I have a daughter? She looks just like her mother. She's at college. A junior this year. She's all I have left."

It all started clicking into place. Fuentes being hired to threaten Carrie to intimidate the commissioner. With Carrie gone, his daughter was the next likely leverage someone could use against him. But who and why? "Who threatened your daughter? Was it the same person who hired Fuentes? Tell me and I can help you."

A knock on the door startled them both. Summer considered ignoring it, but it might be Owen wondering who was in her office without permission. Summer cracked the door and saw the tall, skinny guy who'd been with the commissioner downstairs. "Hi," she said.

"Hello." His smile was perfunctory. "Is the commissioner with you? He's needed downstairs."

She glanced back at the commissioner and saw fear in his eyes, but she wasn't sure if it was residual from the conversation they'd just had or related to the guy standing in front of her.

"We'll be just a bit longer." No way would they be finished with opening statements already. She imagined Faith sitting alone in the gallery of the courtroom watching Owen and wondering where she was. "We'll be down in a few minutes."

She moved to shut the door, but the man raised a hand and blocked it from closing. "I need you both to come with me. Now. It's urgent."

Summer's stomach clenched, and she didn't need to see Carrie Adams jumping up and down behind him, waving her arms, to know this guy was trouble. "Commissioner, talk to me. Who is this guy?"

"Don't let him in." The commissioner's voice was shaky but adamant. And then he surprised her by pressing his hands together and saying, "Rose, don't let anything happen to our daughter."

The guy at the door wasn't giving up that easy. He pushed against the door, and Summer slid backward trying to hold it in place. Would he really try something right here in the courthouse? She considered her options and, since she'd already made a fool of herself once, she figured she may as well go all the way. "Help!" She yelled louder the second time. "Please help!"

❖

Owen strode quickly through the back hallway to the door that led into Judge Whalen's court, but when she reached for the door handle, it opened from the other side and Faith and Dalton were standing in front of her.

"Faith," she said. "I was coming to look for you."

"Mom's in trouble."

"She insisted we had to find you," Dalton said. "I'll try to hold her seat. Judge said she's finishing up reviewing the pretrial motions and she'll be ready to go in about fifteen minutes."

"Thanks, Dalton." Owen waited until he ducked back into the courtroom. "Faith, do you know where your mom is right now?"

She shook her head. "I've tried texting and calling, but she doesn't answer. I know it sounds stupid, but I can tell when something's wrong."

Owen placed a hand on each of Faith's shoulders. "It doesn't sound stupid. It sounds like you have a really strong connection. Can you tap into it now and tell me if she's still in the building?"

Faith closed her eyes, and in that moment, Owen wondered if this was what Summer looked like as a little girl. Had she felt different because she had a superpower no one else could understand? She never wanted Faith to feel that way, and she wished she could take back the hurtful words she'd said to Summer. She vowed she would as soon as she found her. "That's right, Faith. You've got this. Let me know what you see."

"Looks like an office. There's someone with her. I think they're in the building."

Adams. Had she been right all along? Had Adams hired Fuentes to kill his wife? If so, he could be dangerous, and Summer was somewhere in the building with him. In an office. Could they be in her office? Besides the war room where they'd done their trial prep, it was the only other office in the building Summer would be familiar with, so they may as well start there.

Owen crouched down so she was level with Faith. "Faith, I need you to go back in the courtroom and find Mary—she was with me this morning. Tell her I said to do whatever she needs to do, but she needs to get the judge to hold off on starting the trial until I get back. Can you do that?"

Faith nodded. "Are you going to find my mom?"

"Yes. And I won't let anything happen to her. I promise."

As soon as Faith cleared the door back into the courtroom, Owen took off running back to the jury room where she'd left Kira a few minutes ago, thankful to find her still there.

"Hey," Kira said. "I'm sorry about earlier. I—"

"Are you carrying right now?" Owen blurted out.

"Yes."

"Follow me." Owen took off and hoped Kira was behind her. She ran down the back hallway, out the door into the main hall and dodged her way through the crowd. The elected district attorney had a private elevator. Mia had given her the code once when she was working on a special project for her. She hadn't used it in over a year, but she prayed it hadn't changed. She skidded to a stop in front of the elevator and punched in the code, jamming her fist in the air when the doors opened. She stepped in and glanced back at Kira, who was a few steps behind. "Come on."

Kira made it on board as the doors closed, and after catching her breath, asked. "Mind telling me where we're going?"

"My office. I think Summer's in trouble, and I think she's there with someone."

"You think or you know?"

"Look, I know it sounds crazy. This is your chance to make up for this morning. Don't do anything or say anything unless I ask you to. Just be my backup. Okay?"

"Okay."

They spent the next few moments in silence until the elevator dinged its arrival on the eleventh floor. When the doors opened, Owen took off running, with Kira close behind her. The minute she turned down the hallway toward her office, she heard Summer's voice yelling for help. She pumped her legs faster and yelled, "We're coming!" as loud as she could, praying she would get there in time, but when she pulled within a few feet of the door, the cries had stopped.

The door was standing wide open and she edged along the wall to stay out of sight. Kira appeared behind her and followed her lead. When she was close to the opening, she risked a peek through the doorjamb. "What the hell?" She stepped around the door and walked into her office. Commissioner Adams was standing in front of her desk with one foot on the back of a man lying facedown on the ground. She didn't see anyone else in the room, but she felt Summer's presence and a second later, Summer popped out from behind the door brandishing a stapler, which she promptly dropped to the ground.

"You found us."

Owen pulled Summer into her arms and held her tight while Kira cuffed the guy Commissioner Adams had apparently wrestled to the ground. "I was so worried."

"Me too."

"I'm sorry I was an ass."

"I know." Summer leaned back in her arms and Owen

could see the broad smile on her face. "It's probably going to happen again, but I love you anyway."

"I'm counting on it."

CHAPTER EIGHTEEN

Summer stood on the patio of Nan's house surveying the small group gathered in the backyard. Mary was lounging in a chair drinking a virgin margarita while her husband, Jack, set the table. Owen and Faith were taking turns flipping burgers on the grill. She glanced around wondering where Nan was when she appeared from behind her and slipped an arm around her waist.

"You can quit calling it 'Nan's house.'"

"You really shouldn't read people's thoughts without their permission."

"Let me know when you figure out how to tune out the people you love."

"Point taken." At that moment, Owen looked up from the grill and waved. Summer waved back, thinking no one on earth looked as cute in an apron as her girlfriend.

"She's special," Nan said. "Like Charlie special."

The statement made Summer go all misty-eyed. "You're right about that."

"I'm right about a lot of things, and one of them is this house. That high-rise of hers sounds nice, but you both will always be welcome here, and when I'm gone, this place will be yours. Charlie and I discussed it. Besides, I'm counting on you to keep this garden in tip-top shape."

Summer spent a moment imagining Owen and Faith grilling burgers on the weekends, and the three of them hanging out in the backyard until the sun went down. Okay, chances were good that the moment Faith became a teenager she'd want nothing to do with either of them, but there was no harm in dreaming.

"Dinner's ready," Owen called out, waving a spatula in the air.

After they'd dug into the burgers, fresh grilled corn, and Charlie's favorite potato salad, Nan asked for a rundown of the case. "I read the article in the paper three times and I'm still not entirely sure what happened." She pointed at Summer. "This one told me you'd fill me in."

Mary threw her hands up. "Don't ask me. I wasn't in the room when these two decided to take down the bad guy. Owen?"

"I showed up just as the dust settled. Summer, it's all you."

Summer laughed. "Fine, but feel free to chime in. About six months ago, Commissioner Adams discovered there was a major structural issue with the Trinity River Project. A large part of the roadway planned for the development was going to be situated in a flood plain. If the information became public, investors would pull their funding and the project would fail."

"Couldn't they just put the road in somewhere else?" Faith asked.

"Not without chopping up the lots they had designated for the luxury condos both he and Mayor Heller were funding."

"Ah," Jack said. "Money—the quintessential motivator."

"It was for Heller, but Adams actually has a conscience. He made the mistake of telling Heller he was going to go to the city council with the report. Heller's entire candidacy was wrapped up in getting this project rammed through, and if it failed, his reelection prospects and future political prospects in general were dim." Summer nudged Owen. "Your turn."

"Heller hatched a plan to get Adams to keep his mouth shut," Owen said. "Heller has this guy who works for him, Daniels. He's a fixer. He found Fuentes, a guy with prior burglary convictions and dying of cancer. He pays Fuentes to break into the Adamses' house, but Fuentes was only supposed to scare Mrs. Adams, to send a message to the commissioner that he should back off any ideas he had about exposing the flaw in the project. But Fuentes isn't great with guns, and when Carrie Adams put up a fight, the gun went off and he panicked and shot her twice more."

"Here's what I don't get," Nan said, "Why didn't Adams go to the cops right then?"

"Heller told him Fuentes was fully prepared to tell the police that he'd been hired by Adams to kill his wife," Owen said. "Adams had no way of knowing that wasn't true, and Heller and the police chief are golf buddies. Adams has a lot of pull in the county, but when it comes to city politics and the police department, Heller had him on a string. Plus, Daniels, at the mayor's instruction, threatened Fuentes. He wouldn't let Fuentes take a plea, in order to keep Adams under his thumb for as long as possible. If Fuentes spoke out at all, his family wouldn't see a dime of the money he'd been promised."

"I hope they're all going to jail," Faith said.

"That's the plan," Owen said. "After your mom and Commissioner Adams apprehended Daniels in my office, he started telling us everything he knows about Heller's shady deals. I expect the white-collar crime unit will be busy for a while unraveling it all."

Nan stood and started collecting empty plates. "Exciting stuff. Owen, I can't wait to hear what you're working on next."

Summer exchanged looks with Owen. "Should we tell them?"

Owen slid an arm around her waist. "It's your news to tell."

"Don't keep us in suspense," Mary said.

"Mia offered me a permanent position at the DA's office. 'Officially,' I'll be a jury consultant. Unofficially, I'll be your resident psychic medium."

Owen led a toast, and everyone raised a glass and called out congratulations to Summer's new job.

Later, after Mary and Jack left, and Faith was in bed, and Nan was in her room watching *Grey's Anatomy* reruns, Summer asked Owen to join her back out on the patio.

"I'd like to think you brought me out here so we could kiss under the stars," Owen said, "But I have a feeling it's something else. How are my mind-reading skills?"

Summer pulled her close. "Your mind-reading skills are spot-on, although I do want the kissing part too."

"What's up?"

"Mia did offer me the job, but I haven't given her an answer yet."

"Really? I figured it was a done deal."

"I want to make sure you won't mind having me around at work and at home. I know I can be a lot. Me, Nan, Faith, and the spirits—we're a package deal. If it's too much, I completely understand."

Summer locked eyes with Owen, ready for whatever answer she gave and confident they would find a way to work it out. She didn't have to wait long. Owen slid her arms around her waist, pulled her tight, and whispered in her ear, "I want you completely—home, work, wherever. I love Nan, Faith, and even the spirits, but you, Summer Byrne? I love you most of all."

About the Author

Carsen Taite's goal as an author is to spin tales with plot lines as interesting as the cases she encountered in her career as a criminal defense lawyer. She is the award-winning author of over twenty novels of romance and romantic intrigue, including the Luca Bennett Bounty Hunter series, the Lone Star Law series, and the Legal Affairs romances.

Books Available From Bold Strokes Books

A Far Better Thing by JD Wilburn. When needs of her family and wants of her heart clash, Cass Halliburton is faced with the ultimate sacrifice. (978-1-63555-834-0)

Body Language by Renee Roman. When Mika offers to provide Jen erotic tutoring, will sex drive them into a deeper relationship or tear them apart? (978-1-63555-800-5)

Carrie and Hope by Joy Argento. For Carrie and Hope, loss brings them together but secrets and fear may tear them apart. (978-1-63555-827-2)

Detour to Love by Amanda Radley. Celia Scott and Lily Andersen are seatmates on a flight to Tokyo and by turns annoy and fascinate each other. But they're about to realize there's more than one path to love. (978-1-63555-958-3)

Ice Queen by Gun Brooke. School counselor Aislin Kennedy wants to help standoffish CEO Susanna Garry and her troubled teenage daughter become closer—even if it means risking her own heart in the process. (978-1-63555-721-3)

Masquerade by Anne Shade. In 1925 Harlem, New York, a notorious gangster sets her sights set on seducing Celine, and new lovers Dinah and Celine are forced to risk their hearts, and lives, for love. (978-1-63555-831-9)

Royal Family by Jenny Frame. Loss has defined both Clay's and Katya's lives, but guarding their hearts may prove to be the biggest heartbreak of all. (978-1-63555-745-9)

Share the Moon by Toni Logan. Three best friends, an inherited vineyard, and a resident ghost come together for fun, romance, and a touch of magic. (978-1-63555-844-9)

Spirit of the Law by Carsen Taite. Attorney Owen Lassiter will do almost anything to put a murderer behind bars, but can she get past her reluctance to rely on unconventional help from the alluring Summer Byrne and keep from falling in love in the process? (978-1-63555-766-4)

The Devil Incarnate by Ali Vali. Cain Casey has so much to live for, but enemies who lurk in the shadows threaten to unravel it all. (978-1-63555-534-9)

Secret Agent by Michelle Larkin. CIA Agent Peyton North embarks on a global chase to apprehend rogue agent Zoey Blackwood, but her commitment to the mission is tested as the sparks between them ignite and their sizzling attraction approaches a point of no return. (978-1-63555-753-4)

Journey to Cash by Ashley Bartlett. Cash Braddock thought everything was great, but it looks like her history is about to become her right now. Which is a real bummer. (978-1-63555-464-9)

Liberty Bay by Karis Walsh. Wren Lindley's life is mired in tradition and untouched by trends until social media star Gina Strickland introduces an irresistible electricity into her off-the-grid world. (978-1-63555-816-6)

Scent by Kris Bryant. Nico Marshall has been burned by women in the past wanting her for her money. This time, she's determined to win Sophia Sweet over with her charm. (978-1-63555-780-0)

Shadows of Steel by Suzie Clarke. As their worlds collide and their choices come back to haunt them, Rachel and Claire must figure out how to stay together and, most of all, stay alive. (978-1-63555-810-4)

The Clinch by Nicole Disney. Eden Bauer overcame a difficult past to become a world champion mixed martial artist, but now rising star and dreamy bad girl Brooklyn Shaw is a threat both to Eden's title and her heart. (978-1-63555-820-3)

The Last First Kiss by Julie Cannon. Kelly Newsome is so ready for a tropical island vacation, but she never expects to meet the woman who could give her her last first kiss. (978-1-63555-768-8)

The Mandolin Lunch by Missouri Vaun. Despite their immediate attraction, everything about Garet Allen says short-term, and Tess Hill refuses to consider anything less than forever. (978-1-63555-566-0)

Thor: Daughter of Asgard by Genevieve McCluer. When Hannah Olsen finds out she's the reincarnation of Thor, she's thrown into a world of magic and intrigue, unexpected attraction, and a mystery she's got to unravel. (978-1-63555-814-2)

Veterinary Technician by Nancy Wheelton. When a stable of horses is threatened, Val and Ronnie must work together against the odds to save them and maybe even themselves along the way. (978-1-63555-839-5)

16 Steps to Forever by Georgia Beers. Can Brooke Sullivan and Macy Carr find themselves by finding each other? (978-1-63555-762-6)

All I Want for Christmas by Georgia Beers, Maggie Cummings & Fiona Riley. The Christmas season sparks passion and love in these stories by award-winning authors Georgia Beers, Maggie Cummings, and Fiona Riley. (978-1-63555-764-0)

From the Woods by Charlotte Greene. When Fiona goes backpacking in a protected wilderness, the last thing she expects is to be fighting for her life. (978-1-63555-793-0)

Heart of the Storm by Nicole Stiling. For Juliet Mitchell and Sienna Bennett a forbidden attraction definitely isn't worth upending the life they've worked so hard for. Is it? (978-1-63555-789-3)

If You Dare by Sandy Lowe. For Lauren West and Emma Prescott, following their passions is easy. Following their hearts, though? That's almost impossible. (978-1-63555-654-4)

Love Changes Everything by Jaime Maddox. For Samantha Brooks and Kirby Fielding, no matter how careful their plans, love will change everything. (978-1-63555-835-7)

Not This Time by MA Binfield. Flung back into each other's lives, can former bandmates Sophia and Madison have a second chance at romance? (978-1-63555-798-5)

The Found Jar by Jaycie Morrison. Fear keeps Emily Harris trapped in her emotionally vacant life; can she find the courage to let Beck Reynolds guide her toward love? (978-1-63555-825-8)

Aurora by Emma L McGeown. After a traumatic accident, Elena Ricci is stricken with amnesia, leaving her with no recollection of the last eight years, including her wife and son. (978-1-63555-824-1)